No one understands . . . not even her own twin.

"Jessica," Elizabeth said softly, gently, "I know you feel really strongly that there's a spirit protecting you."

"Yes!" This was good. Elizabeth was on her side. "He's so real, Liz—there's no way I could be imagining him."

Elizabeth's eyes were moist. "But Jess, maybe . . . maybe instead of believing he's real, the best thing to do would be to move forward . . . and accept that Nick's not coming back."

The words were like a steely slap in Jessica's face. She jerked her trembling, ice-cold hands out of her sister's grasp and clenched them into fists.

"How can you say that?" she shrieked. "You, of all people!" Jessica stared furiously into Elizabeth's wide eyes. "I *trusted* you, Liz. All this time I waited for you to come home because I thought you would believe me! I thought you'd be on my side!"

"Jess, I *am* on your side," Elizabeth said in a meek, small voice.

"No, you're not!" Jessica rose to her feet, propelled by anguish and rage. She jabbed an accusing finger in her sister's face. "You think I've gone insane, just like everyone else! But I'm *not* crazy! I'm *not!*"

Bantam Books in the Sweet Valley University series.
Ask your bookseller for the books you have missed.

And don't miss these Sweet Valley
University Thriller Editions:

Visit the Official Sweet Valley Web Site on the Internet at:

http://www.sweetvalley.com

SWEET VALLEY UNIVERSITY®

You're Not My Sister

Written by
Laurie John

Created by
FRANCINE PASCAL

BANTAM BOOKS
NEW YORK · TORONTO · LONDON · SYDNEY · AUCKLAND

RL 8, age 14 and up

YOU'RE NOT MY SISTER
A Bantam Book / May 1999

Sweet Valley High® *and Sweet Valley University*®
are registered trademarks of Francine Pascal.
Conceived by Francine Pascal.

Produced by 17th Street Productions,
a division of Daniel Weiss Associates, Inc.
33 West 17th Street
New York, NY 10011.

ISBN: 0-553-49267-5

Published simultaneously in the United States and Canada

Bantam Books are published by Bantam Books, a division of Random
House, Inc. Its trademark, consisting of the words "Bantam Books" and
the portrayal of a rooster, is Registered in U.S. Patent and Trademark
Office and in other countries. Marca Registrada. Bantam Books, 1540
Broadway, New York, New York 10036.

PRINTED IN THE UNITED STATES OF AMERICA

OPM   0 9 8 7 6 5 4 3 2 1

To Mia Pascal Johansson

Chapter One

I'll never leave you . . . you're not alone . . . you're safe, Jessica. . . .

The angel hovered over her, a featureless silhouette that radiated a blindingly bright light. He leaned forward, reached out a hand to stroke her face. . . .

Jessica Wakefield opened her eyes with a start. Sunlight streamed through the windows of . . . her old bedroom at home? She blinked a few times to make sure it was really real. Yes, she was in her old bed, tucked into her old, pink-flowered sheets.

Her father was standing by her bed, looking down at her with an anxious expression. Was he the angel she'd seen in her dream?

Her eyes adjusting to the light, Jessica strained to scan the room. But there was no sign of the mysterious guardian angel. All she saw was the pink-and-white furniture that had surrounded her

1

the whole time she was growing up, scattered in the distance like miniatures in a dollhouse. Other shadows floated through the air, like the ghosts of old childhood memories. But if they were real people, Jessica was too dizzy to make them out.

With an effort, her dry, parched lips formed words. "Wh-What am I doing here?" Jessica's voice sounded like a faraway echo to her own ears.

A hazy figure emerged from the shadows, the blur of her features resolving into Mrs. Wakefield's familiar face. Jessica felt an inexplicable lump rise in her throat as her mother sat down on the edge of her bed.

Alice Wakefield reached out her hand to smooth Jessica's hair, gently picking through the tangles with expert fingers. Her hand felt cool and soothing on Jessica's scalp. "Shhh, honey, you're home now. Everything's going to be all right."

Jessica felt her lip trembling. Something must *not* be all right for her mother to be talking like this; for her father's face to be so grave, almost pained. "Mommy," she found herself saying in a small, choked voice. "What *happened?*"

"We came up to school when it was time for you to go, and we brought you back with us," Mrs. Wakefield explained softly. "Don't you remember?"

Jessica hesitated. Her parents' faces looked so sad, so pitying, she wanted to give the right answer. But her head was spinning. It was all so much to take in at once. *Time for you to go*—what did that mean? Was it summer already?

"I—I guess," she said finally, feeling over-whelmed. Of course her mother had to be telling her the truth. And she had to have made it home somehow since . . . well, here she was.

So how come she couldn't remember how she got here?

Elizabeth Wakefield blinked back tears as she bent over the suitcase she was unpacking. She couldn't stand to look into her twin sister's wide, frightened eyes anymore.

Seeing Jessica sink into weeks of deep depression was painful enough, but the past few days had been pure torture—Jessica would be incoherent one minute, lucid the next. Now she seemed not to remember the day of packing and driving home at all, although Mrs. Wakefield had been patiently recounting the events for a good ten minutes.

Elizabeth lifted a pink spaghetti-strap tank top out of the suitcase and folded it neatly in the top drawer of Jessica's bureau. *Breaking down crying isn't going to do Jess any good,* she reminded herself sternly. *I have to be strong for Mom and Dad's sake.*

Mrs. Wakefield was stroking Jessica's golden hair. "Don't worry about trying to understand right now. Just rest, sweetie."

"But what about school?" Jessica asked. "When do I have to go back?"

3

Elizabeth winced as she slipped a red cocktail dress onto a hanger. Obviously Jessica had blanked out on getting expelled from SVU for plagiarism. Of course, it hadn't been Jessica's fault—in her mental state, she was oblivious to the fact that she'd copied some notes into her philosophy paper directly from other books. If anyone was to blame, it was Elizabeth herself, for insisting that Jessica buckle down and write a paper when she obviously wasn't in any condition to focus on her work.

"You don't have to worry about school—or anything else," Mrs. Wakefield said reassuringly. "You're going to be staying here for a while. We'll take care of you, get you whatever you want."

"Is it like . . . like a vacation?" Jessica asked in a heartbreaking, almost childlike voice.

There was a long silence. Finally the twins' father cleared his throat, his jaw set in a grim line. "Yes," Ned Wakefield said thickly. "Yes, honey, it's kind of like a vacation."

Elizabeth felt herself tearing up again. She reached into Jessica's closet to hang up some dresses, grateful that her parents couldn't see her face.

Pull yourself together, she ordered herself, bending to unlock a trunk. After all her ill-fated attempts to force Jessica back into the normal rhythms of her life backfired, Elizabeth had resolved to detach herself from her sister's life before she drove her sister further away. Sorority dinners, parties, picnics . . . it would have been laughable that Elizabeth actually thought any of those trivial little rituals would snap Jessica out of her funk. It *would* have been—if they hadn't helped push her twin over the edge. The best thing she could do for her sister now was to keep her distance.

"Where's Liz?" Jessica asked suddenly, as if picking up on her twin's thoughts.

Elizabeth straightened up from the trunk with an armful of T-shirts. *What do I say?* she wondered nervously, her throat constricting.

"Elizabeth is here for you, just like we are, Jessica," Mrs. Wakefield supplied. She planted a maternal kiss on Jessica's forehead. "And Steven will be up in a minute, as soon as he's done unpacking the car," she added, referring to the twins' older brother.

"We all want you to know that you can stay home for as long as you want," Mr. Wakefield said. "As long as it takes for you to feel better." Elizabeth could tell how hard it was for her father to keep the emotion out of his voice.

"OK," Jessica agreed, her eyes still wide and unfocused.

Elizabeth fought the urge to throw her arms around her sister and sob. Instead she bent over the trunk. It was so unreal that this was happening. Sorting through the wildly colored piles of miniskirts, tank tops, and short shorts, Elizabeth wondered how these bright, flirty clothes could belong to the waifish, unkempt girl swimming in rumpled pajamas on the bed.

5

Elizabeth felt like kicking herself as she smoothed a blue baby tee into a perfect flat square. She'd always been the grounded one, the stable, practical one, while her wild, adventurous twin flew off in a million directions. Elizabeth should have known that Jessica needed help—*real* help, not just transparent attempts to cheer her up.

But how could I have seen this coming? Elizabeth argued with herself, shouldering another armload of dresses. For all her energy, her volatility, Jessica was, deep down, as resilient as Teflon. She'd weathered a lot of storms in her eighteen-year life—like a turbulent, quickly annulled marriage to Mike McAllery and brushes with death with her cop boyfriend, Nick Fox—but she'd always bounced back.

But this time was different. This time Jessica wasn't . . . well, she wasn't herself.

It had been hard enough for Jessica to accept that Nick's testimony against vicious cop killer Clay DiPalma would force him to enter the witness protection program, in case Clay's thugs sought revenge. But before Nick even had a chance to go into hiding, he'd been brutally gunned down.

All at once Jessica's world had come crashing down. Since Nick was killed, the spark had gone out of her eyes.

Ordinarily it was nearly impossible for strangers to tell the tan, blond twins apart. But right now

Jessica bore only a passing resemblance to Elizabeth—or to herself. The pasty, glassy-eyed girl lying listlessly in bed was just a faint shadow of Jessica Wakefield.

Jessica watched Elizabeth bustle around the room, arranging all her things, and struggled to make sense of what was going on. Now that her eyes had adjusted to the afternoon light, she could see suitcases strewn all around the room. And what had her father said—*as long as it takes . . . ?*

Jessica frowned. She still wasn't sure exactly why she was home, but it looked as if she was going to be staying for a while.

"Well, I guess that's OK," she murmured aloud, almost in a whisper. At least, it was as OK as anything could seem right now. Since Nick had been . . . gone, it wasn't as if she was having any fun at school anyway. Without Nick, everything she'd once enjoyed about her life seemed empty. She'd even considered finding a way out . . . to go to be with Nick forever. Someone had stopped her before it was too late—but who was it? Her guardian angel? Maybe.

She'd actually seen him once—at least, she thought she had. He had been hiding in the bushes outside her dorm, watching her. And that had been . . . when? The day she'd been expelled? Yes. She'd caught a glimpse of him briefly, but not long enough see his face.

Jessica chewed her lip anxiously. Would her angel know to find her here? He had to—angels saw everything, didn't they? He'd *better* find her—she was counting on him. Knowing that someone was watching over her . . . it was all that was keeping her going.

"Don't cry, sweetheart. Everything's going to be all right." Jessica turned wondering eyes onto her mother, who reached out to wipe a stray tear off her cheek. Jessica hadn't even noticed it fall. In fact, she'd forgotten her parents were still there in the room with her. What was *wrong* with her? Why did she feel so disconnected from everything—even herself?

"Everything's going to be *fine*, Jessica," Mr. Wakefield echoed. "You're going to get the help you need—don't worry about anything. You're being well taken care of."

Bells chimed in Jessica's head. They knew! They understood!

She sat up in bed eagerly. "Oh, I know I'm being taken care of!" she agreed excitedly.

Her parents' faces lifted a little. Elizabeth, hovering toward the back of the room, was watching her closely. Encouraged, Jessica went on. "I know I've only seen my guardian angel a couple of times, but I know he's watching over me *all* the time. I can feel him around me."

Beaming, she glanced around at her family. Her smile faded, and Jessica fell back against the pillows.

Her father looked pained. Her mother's lower lip was quivering. And Elizabeth had turned away, busying herself with something in the closet. The only sound in the room was the shriek of wire hangers scraping along the closet rod.

"She finally drifted off," Mrs. Wakefield reported as she entered the kitchen. Mr. Wakefield pulled out a chair for her at the kitchen table, and she dropped into her seat with an air of weariness. Across the table, Elizabeth flashed her mother a tiredly supportive smile.

"You were great with her today, Mom," Steven Wakefield said encouragingly at Elizabeth's elbow. "I know how tough it was for you."

Mr. Wakefield stood behind his wife and started massaging her shoulders. Mrs. Wakefield let her face fall forward as her husband kneaded her neck. "It's tough for all of us. You should have heard her when she started talking about her guardian angel."

"I wonder where she got that." Steven shook his head.

Elizabeth wrapped her hands around the mug of tea she was holding, vaguely comforted by its warmth against her palms. She felt as if she should be the one with an explanation. After all, she was the one who saw Jessica every day—she was supposed to be keeping an eye on her twin.

"Well," Mr. Wakefield said sadly, "I called the

9

doctor and set up an appointment." After a pause he added, almost to himself, "I never expected this."

"None of us did," Mrs. Wakefield assured him, reaching up to pat the hand that rested on her shoulder.

But they weren't with Jess all the time—I was, Elizabeth berated herself. *I should have called Mom and Dad sooner. As soon as she stopped going out, lost her appetite, stopped caring about her appearance . . . But I just kept pushing her, pressuring her.*

The whole mess with the philosophy paper might never have happened if Elizabeth hadn't stupidly insisted it would do Jessica good to throw herself into her schoolwork. Maybe with Elizabeth's support, instead of expulsion Jessica could actually have taken a leave of absence to get the help she needed. But now it was too late.

"Elizabeth, when did you first start noticing a change?" her mother asked suddenly, as if reading Elizabeth's mind.

Elizabeth swallowed hard. "I don't know," she said tersely. "I'm sorry—I just wasn't looking out for her as well as I should have been."

"Nobody's saying that, Liz," Mr. Wakefield interjected.

"We just want to understand how this happened," Mrs. Wakefield insisted. "I know Nick's death was terribly hard on Jessica, but what could have caused her to react like that?"

Well, it couldn't have helped that I kept trying to fast-forward her through the mourning process, Elizabeth thought morosely.

"You must have seen *some* early signs," Mr. Wakefield prompted. "I know it's difficult, but just try to think back. It would really help us know what to tell the doctor."

Elizabeth was beginning to feel defensive. Obviously her parents *did* expect her to have all the answers. "I mean, of course I noticed that she changed after Nick's death, but . . ." Elizabeth stared at the table, unable to meet her family's gaze. "I had a lot of other things going on in my life, OK? How was I supposed to know this would happen?"

"Liz, calm down," Steven said in his knowing, older-brother voice. "We're all really stressed out."

Mr. Wakefield held up his hands placatingly. "We just thought since you're the closest one to her that if anyone would have seen this coming—"

Hot tears filled Elizabeth's eyes. Before she knew what she was doing, she had sprung out of her seat.

"Look, I admit it—I messed up!" she cried. "I *should* have seen it coming, and I didn't! There, are you happy now? It's all my fault!"

Mrs. Wakefield's face crumpled. "Elizabeth, please, we're not saying—"

Her mother's pained expression just fed Elizabeth's guilt. "I know, but you're *thinking* it!"

Tears were streaming down her face. She realized her knees were shaking. "I wasn't there for Jessica—I let everyone down! Well, I'm sorry; I can't do everything right all the time!"

"Elizabeth, keep your voice down." Mr. Wakefield's tone had turned stern. "We don't want to wake Jessica up, and this isn't helping anyone."

"Of course not. *Nothing* I do helps!" Elizabeth grabbed the sweater draped over the back of her chair and started pulling it over her arms. "In fact, maybe I should just leave before I do any more damage!"

All of a sudden she couldn't stand being trapped in that house, surrounded by all the heartbreaking reminders of what a failure she was as a sister. She had to get back to campus, where she could just concentrate on her own life, and not be responsible for anyone else.

She strode through the kitchen door and out to the front hall. Behind her, she heard footsteps and Mr. Wakefield's voice calling, "Elizabeth, get back here. We're all under a lot of pressure—"

At the front door Elizabeth whirled around. "Dad, you have *no* idea how much pressure I'm under. Everybody"—her voice broke—"everybody always expects me to be *perfect,* and I can't! It's hard enough dealing with *my* life without taking care of Jessica too!"

Her father's shoulders slumped. "Fine, Elizabeth. Go live your life."

A knot of pure shame was lodged in

Elizabeth's throat. Wordlessly she picked up the overnight bag she'd left by the door and walked out of the Wakefield house.

Jessica opened her eyes and saw only darkness. It took a minute before the infinite blanket of black softened into indistinct shapes and shades of gray. In another minute those shapes resolved into the familiar pattern of the objects of her old room on Calico Drive. *I'm home,* Jessica recalled, the weight of her depression settling over her as she returned to consciousness.

Only something was different. A black mass loomed at the foot of her bed, heaving. Jessica reached over and switched on her nightstand light, then let out a sigh of relief.

"Prince Albert, you scared me," she whispered. The Wakefields' golden retriever lifted his head and thumped his tail against the bedspread in response.

"C'mere, boy." Jessica patted the mattress by her pillows. The dog obediently stretched out his legs and trotted across the bed into her open arms.

"Oh, that's a good boy," Jessica cooed, stroking the dog's warm folds of fur as Prince Albert licked her face. "Who's a good doggy?" She squeezed the dog's warm, solid body and felt almost moved by the fact that he didn't shy away. It was so nice to have a living, breathing presence beside her— someone who just wanted simple, natural affection.

"You're, like, the only one who still acts normal

13

around me, Albert," Jessica said, scratching the dog's fluffy neck. "You know I'm the same person I always was, right?"

In response Prince Albert let out a wide yawn, punctuated by a little squeak. Jessica chuckled.

"Thanks, pal. I knew you did. Nobody else does, though." She leaned over to nuzzle the soft spot between the dog's ears. "See, I keep seeing this . . . well, I'm pretty sure it's my guardian angel," she went on, lowering her voice. "He watches over me, protects me so I don't get hurt."

Prince Albert cocked his head quizzically, as if he were considering Jessica's words.

"OK, I know it sounds kind of weird," Jessica admitted, "but I know I'm not imagining him. You believe me, don't you?"

Just then Prince Albert barked sharply and jumped off the bed. He bounded to the window and leaped onto his hind legs, pressing his front paws against the pane.

"What is it, Albert?" Jessica exclaimed, following the barking dog to the window. She scanned the Wakefields' darkened backyard, the glittering pool, the rustling tree leaves. Then she saw him.

A dark figure stood under a tree in the yard. His features were obscured by shadow, but she knew right away who it was.

"My angel," she whispered. Prince Albert had seen him and heard him too. He *was* real. If only she could see his face . . .

14

Jessica opened the window and leaned out. "Come closer!" she called out the window. "Let me see you!"

She gestured excitedly, and he took a step closer. Her heart swelled. Finally he was ready to reveal himself. . . .

"Jessica, what's going on? What's wrong?" Her father's voice, from the doorway, startled Jessica. She whirled and saw Mr. and Mrs. Wakefield; she was in her nightgown while he was still knotting the sash of his bathrobe.

"Come quick! The angel! *There!*" Jessica pointed triumphantly to the window.

But when she looked out into the yard, the figure had vanished. Confused, Jessica let her pointing arm drop. "He was right there . . . ," she whispered.

Her parents had come up behind her. She felt her father's hands on her arms. "It's two in the morning, sweetheart," he said in a reasonable voice. "You must have had a bad dream."

"Why don't you try to get some sleep, honey?" her mother chimed in softly. They were gently leading her back to bed now. Jessica kept shaking her head.

"But I was awake," she insisted, lying limply back against her pillows. "He was really here. Prince Albert saw him too!"

She saw her parents exchange looks across the bed. "We'll talk about it in the morning," Mrs. Wakefield said quietly, pulling the comforter up around Jessica's shoulders. "Good night, dear."

Mr. Wakefield switched off the light, and they all filed out, even Prince Albert. Jessica was alone in the darkness again, staring up at a ceiling she couldn't even see.

He crouched down low to the ground, his shallow breaths slicing the still air. A quick glance around revealed that he was completely obscured by a line of hedges.

That was a close one, he thought, his heartbeat gradually slowing to normal. *If only Jessica hadn't called out!* He'd been casing the place all night, and he had been sure that if he scaled the tree by her window, he could make it into Jessica's room.

I've got to figure out some way to get her alone, without attracting anyone's attention, he thought in frustration. The only reason he was here was to get to Jessica Wakefield. He needed to straighten some things out with her. But he had no idea how he was going to get close to her, with her parents always hovering around.

As he watched, the yellow square of light that was Jessica's window was blotted out, swallowed up by the darkness of the night. He kept his eyes on the spot where the light had been.

"Sweet dreams, Jessica," he said under his breath.

Chapter Two

Just act cool, Todd Wilkins ordered himself, shifting his weight from foot to foot. *Try not to come off like a lovesick geek.*

The students in Dana Upshaw's chamber-music ensemble were spilling out the doors of the campus rehearsal space. Todd felt his chest tightening with anxious excitement. How could he *not* make a fool of himself? He was a nervous wreck. He hadn't seen Dana since their incredible night together, when they had shared all their secret fears and most painful memories. Todd had never felt as close to anyone as he had to Dana that night. It was an overwhelming thing to absorb, but he was sure they were meant to be together forever.

But what if she's not feeling it too? His stomach twisted in knots. Nagged by doubts, he'd raced over to the rehearsal space without calling, hoping to surprise Dana on her way out of cello practice.

Then he saw her. Dana was talking animatedly to a girl holding a flute case. Her dark brown hair was pulled up into a loose bun; stray tendrils spilled out onto her face. She was wearing a white angora sweater that curved in all the right places, over an ankle-length but still slinky black skirt. The crowd of students heading into and out of the building might as well not have existed as far as Todd was concerned.

As she approached, she caught Todd's eye, and her face lit up in a breathless, exuberant smile. Todd's heart felt like an airplane taking off.

"I'll see you later, Jodie," Dana told her flutist friend. Her eyes were locked with his as Dana made her way over through the throng of students.

"Hi," she said when she reached him, her smile still open, yet seductive.

"Hey . . . you look incredible," Todd said, wondering if he should indulge his urge to catch her up in his arms and kiss her until he ran out of breath. *Or would that freak her out?* "This is for you," he added awkwardly, producing the single red rose he'd been holding behind his back.

"Oh, thanks," Dana said, taking the flower and kissing him on the cheek. She smiled up at him through lowered lashes. "I'm glad to see you. I was beginning to wonder why I hadn't heard from you."

Todd took a deep breath. "I guess I just wanted to give it some time to make sure you felt . . . the way I do."

"Which is . . . ?" Dana bit her lip coyly.

"Crazy about you."

Todd wasn't sure who made the first move toward whom, but in an instant they were pressed against each other, and his lips crushed hungrily against Dana's. Her fingers were in his hair and his arms wrapped tightly around her waist.

When they finally pulled apart, gasping for air, Dana's hazel eyes were shining. Todd had no words for how beautiful her flushed face looked. And she was *his*—he knew that now, beyond any shadow of doubt. All his nervousness had fled the moment he swept Dana into his arms.

"You were scared, weren't you?" she said, reading his mind. "Scared that it was too good to be true."

He nodded. "I never opened up to anyone the way I did with you. I was worried I came on too strong."

"But you *are* strong, and that's what I love about you." Dana squeezed his muscular bicep playfully. "And I don't mean big-dumb-jock strong. I mean strong *inside*—because you put all your cards on the table. We've both learned life's too short to play games."

"That's for sure," Todd agreed, a catch in his throat. He'd poured out his heart to Dana about

19

how empty his existence had been since his girl-friend, Gin-Yung Suh, died of a brain tumor. He'd even confessed to Dana what he'd only told his therapist—how afraid he was of being disloyal to Gin-Yung's memory, how scared he was that he would never love anyone again. But he wasn't afraid anymore. The campus might be shrouded in painful memories of Gin-Yung, but with Dana he could rebuild his life and make new memories.

A sly smile crept across Todd's face. "Now what was that *l* word you just used?"

"Hmmm, I can't quite recall." Dana scrunched up her face in a mock-thoughtful expression. "Was it *loofah? Lava? Longitude?*"

"Close enough." Todd drew her face close to his, and their lips merged in a searing kiss.

Todd had cared for Gin-Yung deeply, and Elizabeth Wakefield would always be his first love. But nobody had ever made him feel as much at ease, as *accepted,* as Dana did. He could tell her anything, and she'd just listen and understand. They were totally on the same wavelength. *Totally.*

Dana sighed as she tipped back her head. The small hollow in her milky throat heaved with shallow breaths. "I think that jogged my memory," she admitted, smiling almost shyly. "I love you, Todd."

"I love you too, Dana." Todd gave her waist a squeeze. Just hearing her say the words—and saying them back—made him feel giddy, like a little kid. They kissed again, short but tender this time.

"So," Todd said eagerly, "will you do me the honor of going out with me tomorrow night? I want to take you someplace incredibly nice."

Dana frowned. "*Out?* Tomorrow? I'm not really into that idea."

Todd was bombarded by panic. Confusion. Despair. "Y-You're not?"

"No." Dana's lashes fluttered. "I was kind of hoping we could . . . stay in instead."

Todd felt every muscle in his body relaxing as Dana's lips were raised to his once more. Now he was sure. He and Dana were *definitely* on the same wavelength.

Elizabeth's hand trembled as she reached toward the door of apartment 6B. Her knocks were drowned out by the sound of her heart hammering in her chest. After a second the door opened.

Mike McAllery stood in the open doorway of his apartment, wearing only a white ribbed undershirt and an old, faded pair of jeans. He looked surprised to see her. "Elizabeth," he said, ruffling his already tousled dark hair.

"Hi," she said, inexplicably short of breath. "Could I come in, or . . . is this a bad time?"

"No, no—come on in." Mike held open the door and ushered her inside.

Elizabeth stood, holding her arms, in the small living room as he shut and locked the door behind her. This apartment was a far cry from the lavish place Mike had kept when he lived in the same building as her brother.

All of a sudden she felt awkward, unsure. Their shared concern for Jessica had brought her and Mike together, but when they had met to brainstorm ways to help Jessica, their relationship had grown into something more. What else, Elizabeth wasn't sure yet. But it felt strange to turn to her sister's ex-husband for comfort . . . even if he was the only person who *could* comfort her right now.

Mike turned expectantly toward her. "It's good to see you, Liz. Is everything OK?"

Elizabeth shrugged, utterly inarticulate. "I came straight from my parents' house," she explained. "It was just so tense. I had to get away and get my mind off Jess . . . off everything."

Mike's concerned expression evaporated, and he cocked his head to one side. A grin stretched across his ruggedly handsome face. "Well, I might be able to help with that."

Elizabeth stepped into his outstretched arms. She let her eyes flutter shut, anticipating the electric charge of Mike's touch, which obliterated her awareness of everything and everyone else . . . even Jessica.

Jessica. In spite of herself Elizabeth felt a stab of remorse. Her eyes flew open. "I mean, it's not like I was doing anybody any good anyway," she reasoned aloud. "There really was no reason for me to stay."

Mike wrapped his powerful arms around her waist. "No argument here." He lowered his face to hers.

Elizabeth felt her lips tingle with expectation. This was why she'd come here, the only way to make all the chaos in her mind fall away. Mike's kiss—a kiss that could make a marble statue's knees go weak. Now she could forget all about her sister, lying helplessly on that bed, too dazed to understand that her life had fallen apart. . . .

"I just couldn't take it," Elizabeth found herself saying suddenly. "I mean, you know how full of life Jessica is. It's torture to see her like this."

Mike lifted his head. Elizabeth thought she saw a shadow of what could have been frustration cross his face. But it passed instantly, and he nodded sympathetically. "I can imagine."

"It's not like I'm a bad sister or anything," Elizabeth went on. "I just have *other* stuff going on in my life. You don't think I'm a terrible sister, do you?"

Mike groaned and chucked her under the chin. "You're not a terrible sister. You don't have a terrible bone in your body, Liz. Will you cut this out? You're driving yourself crazy."

Elizabeth sighed. "I know, I know! I just can't help—"

"Liz!" Mike interrupted. "About that . . . *other* stuff you've got going on?"

"Yes, but I . . ."

She didn't get a chance to finish. Mike pressed his lips against hers, sending fire from the crown of her head to the tips of her toes. At that moment Elizabeth felt that she really had escaped all her problems. Nothing existed except her and Mike McAllery.

A loud, crashing noise shattered the tranquil air of Tom Watts's dorm room. Tom looked up from his sociology book and saw his roommate, Danny Wyatt, careen through the door. Danny was slumped forward, leaning all his weight on the doorknob. When he saw Tom, he grinned, his bloodshot eyes narrowing into a squint.

"Heeeyyy, Tom," Danny slurred. "Howzitgoin, maaan?" He lurched forward and staggered over to his bed, where he collapsed in a heap onto his stomach. Tom wrinkled his nose at the rank tequila stench that radiated from his roommate.

"Another wild night, huh?" Tom asked dryly, pushing back his desk chair and getting up to close the door.

"Yeah, me anna bunch of guys from Sigma house were matching shots at that sports bar a coupla blocks off campus." Danny rolled over onto his back and let out a guttural groan. "The room is *spinning,* man."

Tom let out a low whistle. "Dude, you are *wasted.*"

"Correct!" With a gurgling laugh Danny

jabbed his finger up toward the ceiling. "And why the hell shouldn't I be? Isabella's gone—I might as well let myself go!"

Tom sat down on his bed, across from Danny's, surveying his friend sympathetically. Danny had blamed himself when his girlfriend, Isabella Ricci, had unwittingly accepted a PCP-laced cigarette from professional scumbag Clay DiPalma—and plunged off a balcony, ending up with amnesia, if not brain damage. And when Mr. and Mrs. Ricci decided to move Isabella far away from SVU, Danny had started spiraling into despair. This was the third or fourth night in a week he had come back to the room stumbling drunk.

"Listen, Danny, I know you're still hurting over Isabella," Tom said. "But you can't keep trashing your body like this. Believe me, not a day goes by that I don't think about getting Elizabeth Wakefield back. But life goes on, man."

"Easy for you to say!" Danny spluttered. With obvious effort he swung himself up to a sitting position and stared indignantly at Tom. "At least you can still *see* Elizabeth—I'll *never* speak to Izzy again! What am I gonna do, drop by the next time I'm in Switzerland?"

"Switzerland?" Tom echoed thoughtfully.

"Yeah, her parents hate me so much, they dragged her off to some hoity-toity hospital thousands of miles away," Danny said disgustedly.

25

"Izzy's gone, and it's all my fault." He dropped his head into his hands.

Tom's heart contracted in empathy. He knew just how devastated his friend felt. Danny was wrong—it *wasn't* easy for Tom to talk about getting over Elizabeth. He didn't know if he'd ever truly get past their breakup, especially knowing that he'd single-handedly ruined everything. First he'd lied to Elizabeth about sleeping with Dana Upshaw while they were broken up; then he'd gotten so defensive about her self-righteous attitude that he'd called her frigid—among other things he didn't want to remember right now.

In fact, it might actually be easier if Elizabeth *were in Switzerland,* Tom thought bitterly. At least then he wouldn't have to see her . . . hear about her . . . torture himself dwelling on how he had idiotically destroyed their chances of ever getting back together.

Danny jerked his head up suddenly, startling Tom out of the Elizabeth zone. "Whatever, man; it's cool," Danny said unconvincingly, standing up on wobbly legs. "I'm over it. There's plenty of other women out there." He stumbled across the room and bent over in front of the minifridge under Tom's desk. "Hey, do we have any beer left over from that six I got the other night?"

"I think you've had enough, pal," Tom pointed out, knowing Danny wasn't listening. He watched Danny rifle through the fridge and shook his head sadly.

There has to be something I can do to help him, Tom mused. Danny might have given up on Isabella, but Tom was willing to bet he could track her down if he put his mind to it. He didn't want to watch his best friend drink his life away.

And if reuniting Danny and Isabella happened to help Tom forget the wretched mess he'd made with Elizabeth Wakefield, the only girl he'd ever truly loved . . . well, then so much the better.

"Oh, Mike . . . ," Elizabeth whispered, feeling his mouth burn a trail of kisses from her ear down her neck. She ran her fingers almost roughly through his hair, surprised at the force of her own passion.

"Your body is amazing," Mike said in a low, urgent voice. He unbuttoned the top button of her shirt and kissed her collarbone, sending shivers down Elizabeth's spine.

She arched her head back against the sofa pillows. Mike's lips were soft, but at the same time she could feel the sting of his unshaven face against her skin. The sensation was exquisite.

His mouth found hers again, and Elizabeth felt as if she were soaring. Mike's warm hands slid down her back, around her waist, and under her shirt. Almost before she could process what was happening, his fingers had found their way back to the hollow of her spine and were working expertly to unhook her bra.

Alarm sliced through the blissful bubble of pleasure that surrounded Elizabeth. This was going way too far, way too fast. She pushed him away, her breath coming in shallow gasps.

Mike propped himself up on his knuckles and stared down at her in surprise. "What's the matter? Did I do something wrong?"

Elizabeth hesitated. Should she explain that she'd never done *it*—not even with Tom Watts, the ex-boyfriend she'd dated for ages?

In spite of herself she found Tom's words echoing through her head. *Frigid. Old maid.* She cringed, recalling their public shouting match when Tom had accused her of being neurotically uptight. *Just because I resented him sharing with Dana a kind of closeness* we'd *never experienced,* Elizabeth thought, still outraged at the memory. But part of her felt a tiny bit ashamed too.

"Liz? Talk to me," Mike prompted. "Whatever it is, you know you can trust me, don't you?"

"I do; I just . . ." She trailed off, embarrassed—and a little scared—to admit the truth. What would Mike say if he knew she was still a virgin? Would *he* think she was frigid? Or just weird? Obviously Mike was used to dating experienced women, not college girls.

Then again, Elizabeth realized, a creepy feeling

prickling across her skin, *Jessica was a virgin too . . . when she* met *Mike.*

Suddenly Mike's weight on top of her felt crushing. Elizabeth squirmed sideways, wriggling away from him. She extracted her legs, which were tangled with his, and sat up straight on the couch.

"I'm sorry, Mike. I guess I'm just . . . preoccupied. I can't take my mind off Jessica." That wasn't entirely a lie—the thought of her own twin losing her virginity to Mike was definitely a mood killer. "So I think . . . I think it would be better if I just leave."

Mike nodded slowly. "OK, I understand." He sat up beside her and put a comforting arm around her shoulders. "Are you sure you don't want to stay and talk about it?"

Elizabeth laced her fingers nervously in her lap. She could feel how rigid her spine was. "No, thanks, I think I just need to be alone right now." She gave him an abrupt peck on the cheek and stood up. Mike made a move to follow her, but she motioned him to stay put. "That's OK—I can show myself out."

Mike wordlessly studied her face. Tension hung between them in the air, as palpable as their passion had been a few minutes ago. Elizabeth turned and headed toward the door, fumbling with her shirt buttons as she went. All at once she really *couldn't* wait to be alone.

Chapter Three

What am I going to do with myself all day? That was the first thought that ran through Jessica's mind when she opened her eyes. The light of morning glowed through her gauzy curtains. Outside, she could hear the noises of children playing, birds chirping, dogs barking.

But everything seemed small, empty, distant. Jessica felt like a giant in her pink room of dollhouse miniatures, as if she had outgrown the space in the year she'd been gone. Being back at home was like being in a time warp; nothing had changed—Nick might never have even existed.

I used to be happy when I lived here, Jessica reminded herself, staring up at the blank, white ceiling. *What did I do then?* She struggled to summon memories of everything that had seemed like so much fun to her. The beach, the mall, the diner . . . bonfires, parties, sleep overs . . .

Did I ever really do all that stuff? she wondered incredulously. Her high-school world seemed imaginary, like something she'd seen in a movie rather than lived.

But maybe it could come back to me. Maybe Elizabeth remembers. Brightening a little at the thought of her sister, Jessica sat up straight in bed. Maybe they could do some of that silly stuff they used to do in high school, just for old times' sake.

Jessica climbed out of bed and slid her feet into her worn old bedroom slippers. She bounded through the bathroom that joined the twins' bedrooms, feeling more like her old self already. As always, she didn't bother knocking before she threw open the door to Elizabeth's bedroom. "Hey, Liz, what do you say we go to the beach or . . ."

Jessica trailed off. Elizabeth's room was empty, still. The bed was made. There were no traces of her twin. Jessica blinked.

Oh, of course—Liz always gets up early, she realized, relieved. *She must have gone out.*

Jessica padded down to the Wakefields' kitchen, where her mother was slicing strawberries at the counter.

Mrs. Wakefield looked up and smiled widely. "Hi, sweetie! I was just going to make some fruit salad. Can I get you anything?"

"Where's Elizabeth?" Jessica asked.

Mrs. Wakefield's face dropped. "Oh. She . . .

she went back to school, Jess. But she'll be back soon to visit you," she added hastily.

Jessica's mouth formed an O, but no sound came out. Elizabeth . . . *gone*? Hadn't her mother said it was some kind of vacation? It had never occurred to Jessica that the twins wouldn't be staying home *together*. This changed everything.

"So what . . . what am I going to do with myself now?" Jessica asked finally, her own voice sounding small and faraway.

"Oh, don't worry, sweetie; it's all right." Mrs. Wakefield came over and hugged Jessica, patting her back vigorously. "Really, Elizabeth will be back soon, I promise."

Jessica couldn't muster the effort to return her mother's embrace. Her arms hung limply at her sides.

Mrs. Wakefield stepped back to hold Jessica's shoulders at arm's length. "I know! It's an absolutely beautiful day outside. Why don't you go out back and sit by the pool? I bet getting some sun would feel good."

"I guess," Jessica said without enthusiasm. "That sounds OK."

Jessica went to the sliding-glass door that led out to the Wakefields' backyard. She pulled it open and shuffled outside onto the deck. For a moment she was blinded by the brilliant sun beating down relentlessly from a cloudless blue sky. Jessica squinted hard. The surface of the pool was one sheer pane of glaring, reflected light. Everything else was in sharp focus; every blade of grass, every crack in the pale poolside cement seemed to stand out in stark relief. Jessica's skin began to feel clammy under her flannel pajamas.

Quickly Jessica turned and went back inside, yanking the sliding door shut. She wandered back into the kitchen, feeling slightly dazed as her eyes readjusted to the soothing dimness inside.

Mrs. Wakefield looked startled to see her. "What's wrong, Jess?"

Jessica shrugged helplessly. "It's so . . . bright." She stared down at the tiled floor, suddenly spent of her energy. "Maybe I'll just go back to bed for a while."

"Unnnggghhh," Danny Wyatt groaned as he swung himself forward to sit up in bed. "Twelve tequila shots. What was I *thinking?*"

For a moment he sat perfectly still, letting the pit of his stomach catch up with the rest of his body. Then, careful to preserve the delicate equilibrium between his splitting headache, his aching muscles, and the waves of nausea washing over him, Danny swiveled his pounding head to look at his nightstand alarm clock.

1:30 P.M., the red letters jeered. They might as well have added, *You wasteoid.* He'd slept through three classes, including a biology quiz.

Danny's eyes wandered to the glass of water

34

and bottle of aspirin sitting on the nightstand. *Thanks, Tommy,* he thought sheepishly, glancing over at Tom's neatly made bed as he reached for the aspirin. He barely remembered even seeing his roommate last night, but obviously he'd made no secret of the fact that he was plastered.

Danny cringed. *I must have made a huge jackass of myself.* He had a vague recollection of ranting about Isabella, but anything beyond that was a blur. As he gulped down two aspirins, he searched through his foggy impressions of last night, trying to remember. But the effort seemed to intensify the hammer pounding against his temples, so he gave up. *Whatever I said, it was probably humiliating,* he concluded glumly.

As much as Danny wanted to crawl back under the covers, the urge to clean himself up was overpowering. He was still wearing the clothes he'd passed out in. And his parched mouth tasted like he'd been licking the floor of a subway station. Slowly, carefully, Danny hauled his wretched body out of bed and dragged himself to the bathroom.

Reaching for his toothbrush, he caught a glimpse of himself in the mirror. *I didn't know I* had *that many blood vessels in my eyes,* Danny marveled, leaning in close to focus on the fine network of red lines that splintered across his corneas.

"You are a pathetic mess," he told his reflection. "What kind of loser lets a woman turn him into a wreck?"

Danny ran a hand through his close-cropped, dark, curly hair. His talk with Tom was starting to come back to him. *Life goes on*—that was what Tom had said. And as hard as it was for Danny to accept, Tom was right. Isabella wasn't coming back. And Danny couldn't keep beating himself up about it.

I have to get over her, Danny resolved silently to his mirror image. His parents didn't work to pay his tuition so he could drink like a fish and sleep through all his classes. There had to be a better way to deal with losing Isabella—something that didn't involve trying to kill all the relevant brain cells.

And he had to find it soon. Because he never, ever wanted to feel this horrible pulsing, throbbing, excruciating pain in his head again.

"Swiss . . . no, Switzerland," Tom mumbled, backspacing over what he had just typed. "Hospitals."

He clicked the button marked Search and sat back in his desk chair, gazing thoughtfully across the WSVU office as the computer loaded his results. *If the Riccis flew Isabella all the way to Europe,* Tom reasoned, *the hospital must be pretty well-known.* With any luck, he'd be able to track it down on the web.

"I'm taking off, Tom," announced Debbie Seymour, one of the WSVU interns, waving on her way out of the campus TV station office.

"Have a good night—don't work too hard."

"Don't worry; I won't," Tom called out absently as the door slammed shut. It was the truth—although his editorial on campus politics was scheduled to air tomorrow, his notes lay in an untouched pile on his desk. But every time he turned to them, he was confronted with the mental image of Danny's miserable, downtrodden expression.

A new web page popped up. Tom scrolled down, scanning his search results. Almost all the entries were in German and French.

"That's helpful," Tom muttered. He clicked on the first hospital on the list and watched as the screen popped up a picture of a sprawling, white building complex. He scanned the incomprehensible German text on the page until he saw the string of words and digits that were obviously the address and phone number.

Should I call? Tom wondered. *Would I even be able to communicate?* He wasn't exactly in a financial position to ring up every hospital in Switzerland for the heck of it. *This is like looking for a needle in a haystack,* Tom thought in exasperation. *There's got to be a better way.*

He extracted the pencil from behind his ear and tapped it against the blank notepad on his desk. OK—what if this was a news story? The next logical step would be to track down a source close to the subject. The Riccis hadn't wanted *Danny* to know Isabella's whereabouts, but *someone* close to her must have some clues.

Tom leaned back in his desk chair and ran through a mental list of Isabella's confidantes. Jessica Wakefield was probably her best friend. But Jessica had been pretty much out of the loop since Nick died.

He would have loved to offer Elizabeth and her sister a shoulder to lean on. But after the crude, cruel way he'd mocked her in the quad, there was no way Elizabeth would ever want to speak to him, let alone—

OK, don't go there, he told himself. He had the rest of his miserable life to mope about losing Elizabeth.

Leaning over his pad, Tom willed himself to concentrate. After Jessica, Isabella's best friend was . . . Denise Waters? Or . . .

"Lila!" Tom exclaimed, snapping his fingers. It was a no-brainer—he was amazed he hadn't thought of it sooner. Lila Fowler was one of Isabella's closest friends *and* her family came from the same wealthy, sophisticated circles that the Riccis did. If anyone at SVU knew anything about an exclusive Swiss hospital, it would be Lila. And if she didn't . . . well, she was a *much* better schmoozer than he was.

"Hey, Liz!" a chipper female voice called down the corridor of Dickinson Hall.

Elizabeth looked up from her leather backpack, which she was rooting through for her keys, and saw Kaeshi Lin, one of the girls on her floor, waving at her.

"Hey, Kaesh," Elizabeth said. She extracted her key and swung her backpack over her shoulder. "How's it going?"

"Great, since I got a B-plus on my medieval-lit paper." Kaeshi giggled. "I was sweating bullets over that one. Hey, do you know what Jess is up to? She hasn't been in class lately, and I haven't seen her around the dorm either."

Elizabeth kept her face impassive as she turned her key in the lock. "She's taking some time off," she said lightly. The vague excuse rolled more easily off her tongue each time she gave it. Jessica knew so many people—it seemed as if Elizabeth had to explain her twin's absence every time she turned around.

"Oh, cool. Wish I was!" Kaeshi flipped one of her long, black pigtails over her shoulder and flashed Elizabeth a smile. "So is she enjoying herself?"

"Yup," Elizabeth responded mechanically. "Well, I'll see you around!" She opened the door a crack and wedged herself quickly through, not wanting Kaeshi to peer in and see that Jessica's side of the room was completely bare. It was hard keeping Jessica's condition to herself, but the last thing she needed was the entire campus

39

knowing about the Wakefield family crisis.

Elizabeth locked the door behind her and stood for a moment in silence. She still wasn't used to how empty the room felt without Jessica's avalanche of clutter, the heaps of clothes and books and toiletries and . . . *stuff* that her sister habitually left strewn around the bed and floor. Elizabeth had always chastised her sister for living like a pig. But right now she would have liked nothing better than to step on a stray pot of Jessica's lip gloss or find panty hose draped over every available surface in the room. As it was, the bare wooden floorboards and the bed stripped down to a plain white mattress on a gray iron frame reminded Elizabeth of a prison cell.

Elizabeth sat down at her desk, uncapped her yellow highlighter, and found her place in her political-science textbook. *The advent of Communism was heralded by a paradigm shift in . . .*

Out of the corner of her eye she could see the bright, stark white edge of Jessica's mattress. Elizabeth shielded the side of her face with her hand and kept reading. The silence in the room was deafening. She tapped her highlighter against the desk and was startled by how loud it sounded.

Liz, stop reading that snooze-fest of a book and pay attention to me, she could practically hear Jessica saying. *Which dress do you like better, this one or the first one?* Elizabeth had always assumed it would be easier to get her work done without

Jessica bugging her all the time. But the harder she tried to concentrate, the more Elizabeth was acutely aware of her sister's absence.

Elizabeth let out a quavering breath. She grabbed her poli-sci book and dumped it into her backpack, then slung the pack over her shoulder and headed for the door. All of a sudden she couldn't stand to spend another second alone in her dorm room. Without Jessica, the empty side of the room felt deserted. Haunted.

"What does *fondue* mean anyway?" Todd asked, his dark brown eyebrows crinkling together adorably. He leaned over and popped another piece of bread and cheese into Dana's mouth.

"I'm not sure, but I think it's French for yummy," Dana said when she had finished chewing. "I'm stuffed, and I still want to keep eating." They were sitting on cushions on the spacious wooden window seat of the large bay window in Dana's living room. A pot of fondue, a half-eaten baguette, and a bottle of red wine rested between them on the seat. Through the window they could see the sun setting over the green-shrubbed hills, suffusing the landscape in a dusky pink glow. Dana felt as if she were floating on cloud nine.

Todd grinned. "I'm glad you're not one of those water-and-a-salad girls. I hate that. Us jock types need a woman who appreciates a hearty meal." He leaned over to give her a playful kiss on

41

the tip of her nose. Dana sprinted up to clouds ten, eleven, and twelve.

It's so easy *with Todd*, she marveled, reaching for his hand. *So natural, so normal, so honest.* It was so different from her last relationship, with Tom Watts. With Tom, Dana had always known in her heart that she was the one doing all the work, forcing a connection that Tom didn't really want.

"You know, this is really a beautiful house," Todd reflected, gazing out at the view. "I can't believe students can afford to live here."

"The rent's actually not bad, split five ways. The only problem is living with that many roommates." Dana took a delicate sip of her wine. "I mean, they were cool about clearing out tonight when I said I had a date. But normally it's impossible to get any privacy."

Todd craned his head, scanning the room. "But this place is amazing—high ceilings, old-fashioned woodwork. . . ." His eyes met Dana's, twinkling mischievously. "Imagine if we had a whole place like this to ourselves."

Dana nodded enthusiastically, squeezing Todd's hand. "And as long as we're dreaming, let's say no classes, no papers, no tests."

"Yeah, school most definitely does not factor into this equation," Todd agreed. Maneuvering around the dinner things, he slid across the window seat to sit next to Dana. "It would be so cool to ditch the whole campus scene and live like adults. You know, house, job, the works. Fast-forward to our future."

Dana glowed as Todd tenderly wrapped an arm around her shoulders. "That would be incredible."

Tom Watts would never have said anything like that, she couldn't help thinking. *I wasn't included in the picture of his future.* For Tom Watts the future had meant winning back Elizabeth Wakefield, the blond, blue-eyed specter that had loomed over their relationship. With Tom she'd been "on" all the time—putting on an act, in a way—since she had to keep up her guard against Elizabeth.

It was definitely an unfortunate coincidence that Todd used to date Elizabeth too, Dana had to admit. But she honestly didn't feel threatened. Dana knew in her heart that Todd couldn't look at her the way he did if he were still carrying a torch for Elizabeth.

"We could leave behind all the bad memories," she went on, getting inspired. "Everyone who knows us as the people we *used* to be, not who we are now. Wipe the slate clean and start over."

"Amen to that." Todd's light, playful voice had taken on a serious tone. "I can't even tell you how sick I am of people seeing me as the big-jerk-on-campus, hotshot basketball star I was when I

43

got here. That's not the person I'm trying to be at all."

Dana looked up at Todd, moved by how well they understood each other. It was an immense relief to know that she could be honest with Todd—and that meant she could be honest with herself. "The person I want to be," she said softly, "is the person I am when I'm with you."

They gazed deeply into each other's eyes, communicating without words. Then Todd gently brushed her lips with his. Time seemed to stand still as their mouths merged. Dana felt as if her whole body were bathed in the same rosy glow as the sky outside.

"Do you want to show me your room?" Todd asked huskily when they finally separated.

Dana exhaled slowly. Her body was screaming, *Yes! Yes!* But she'd fallen for Todd so quickly. They were still just getting to know each other, and she was savoring the exciting newness of their relationship. With Tom she'd rushed into things, and . . . well, look how well *that* turned out.

"Todd, if it's OK with you, I'd . . . I'd really like to take things slow for now." Dana bit her lip and nervously looked up at Todd. His expression was indistinct now in the dying light.

"If it's OK with me?" Todd repeated with a laugh. He enfolded her in a big bear hug and kissed the top of her head. "Dana, I'm not some

Neanderthal, you know. There's no need to rush things—we've got all the time in the world."

Dana felt a relieved grin spread across her face. Of course Todd wouldn't try to pressure her—she wouldn't have fallen in love with a guy like that. She kissed him again, the words echoing sweetly in her head: *all the time in the world.*

Chapter
Four

"Coming up after the break," enthused the ash-blond woman in the coral blazer, "we'll show you how to make your own air freshener using pinecones and cheesecloth!"

Jessica, slumped on the living-room couch in her bathrobe, lifted the remote control and aimed it squarely at the blond woman's head. With one zap she disappeared, replaced by a man in a fishing boat. Jessica kept pushing the button, flipping channels. There was nothing she really wanted to watch. But the bright flashes of light, the sharp bursts of static, were oddly comforting—almost hypnotic. The TV kept her distracted, kept her mind from tracing the same circles over and over. *The angel is real. . . . I'm not imagining it. . . . But what if I am? . . .*

Suddenly something on the TV screen caught her eye. *Could it be?* . . . Jessica quickly flipped back to the channel. Sure enough, the image of an angel filled the screen. It was a medieval painting; the angel's delicate face and prayer-clasped hands gleamed white against a field of gold.

"More and more people today believe that angels are all around us," a voice-over intoned. "In our troubled modern times, we are all comforted by the idea that there's a spiritual presence in all of our lives, watching over us."

Jessica's jaw hung open. The remote control slipped from her hand.

The screen cut to a gray-haired woman in a denim shirt, wearing large feather earrings and heaps of turquoise beads. "Some Native American cultures believe every person has his or her own spirit guide, a presence that guides us through life."

Jessica covered her mouth with her hands and slid forward to the edge of the couch. Excitement fluttered in her stomach. *I'm* not *imagining things!* she felt like shouting. *If only someone were here to see this!* But her parents were both at work.

". . . and some groups believe the angels in our lives are the spirits of deceased loved ones—like ghosts, but sent down to earth for a benevolent purpose, to protect us. . . ."

Deceased loved ones . . . The cogs of Jessica's mind slowly turned.

"Nick?" Jessica whispered through her fingers, tears welling up in her eyes.

It was all too much to take in at once, too many possibilities to consider. She wished Elizabeth were here. Elizabeth was such a good listener. Maybe if she saw the show, she would believe her. . . .

Jessica bounded upstairs to her room and grabbed the cordless phone on her nightstand. She dialed their room at SVU and tapped her foot anxiously as the phone rang two, three, four times. . . .

"Hi," came Elizabeth's voice.

"Liz, it's me. I'm so glad you—," Jessica began breathlessly.

"We're not here right now," Elizabeth continued, her voice warbling a little on the recording.

"So leave a message," Jessica's chirpy voice chimed in, sounding like a stranger's. Had she really ever been that happy?

"And we'll call you back!" the twins chorused, followed by a shrill beep.

"Liz, it's me," Jessica began again. "Pick up if you're there. Are you there? No? OK, sorry! Listen, I have to tell you something really, really, really exciting, OK?" She paused for breath and realized she was bouncing up and down on her bed. "I saw my angel on TV! I mean, not *my* angel exactly, but they were talking about him. I mean . . . well, he's *real,* Liz! They said lots of people have spirits watching them. I swear, Liz, if you had seen it, you'd understand! Anyway, call me back as soon as you can, and I'll explain the whole thing because I really, really, really need you to believe me, OK? I love you, Liz! Bye!"

Jessica hung up, wiping the sweat off her palms. A smile spread across her face. Elizabeth had been so worried about her lately. She would be relieved to hear Jessica sounding so upbeat. That message would reassure her sister that Jessica had everything under control.

Elizabeth wedged herself through the partially open door of room 28, Dickinson Hall, closed it firmly behind her, and let out a deep sigh. She'd just stopped by her room to drop off her books between women's-studies class and her afternoon coffee date with her best friend, Nina Harper. But already two girls on her floor had stopped her to ask about her twin. Elizabeth shook her head sadly. The fact that so many people cared about Jessica just made it more shocking and strange that she had become so isolated and unstable.

As she unslung her backpack, Elizabeth noticed that the red light on her answering machine was blinking. *Mike,* she thought involuntarily.

She hadn't heard from him since she ran out so abruptly the other day, and she was too embarrassed to call him. But as confused as she was about the relationship—or whatever it was—Elizabeth couldn't help hoping that Mike hadn't given up on her. She pushed play and hovered over the machine, biting her nail anxiously.

Beep. "Liz, it's me. Pick up if you're there. . . ."

Elizabeth's heart gave a spasm. Jessica's voice was shrill, high-pitched, breathless. Elizabeth stood frozen in place as her sister rambled on, a little too quickly to be coherent. She sounded giddy, practically manic. *"My angel . . . my angel . . ."* were the only words Elizabeth could pick out clearly.

". . . need you to believe me, OK? I love you, Liz! Bye!"

All of a sudden Elizabeth felt crushingly lonely. She'd always been part of a pair—as different as she and Jessica were, they were two halves of the same whole. Now her twin was slipping further and further away, losing her grip on reality altogether. With Jessica babbling about seeing angels on TV, Elizabeth knew she was really on her own.

Should I call back? she wondered, halfheartedly gripping the phone receiver without taking it off the hook. *Maybe I'd better not. . . .* After all, she had resolved to keep her distance from her sister— physically *and* emotionally.

But that's just a cop-out, and you know it, a voice in Elizabeth's head taunted her. *You don't* want *to call her back.*

Elizabeth turned away from the phone and wrung her hands together mournfully. That disembodied, incoherent voice on the machine did

51

not belong to her sister. Just the thought of trying to communicate with it filled Elizabeth with dread. It was both depressing and terrifying to hear Jessica in that state.

I'm just not going to think about it any more right now, Elizabeth resolved. She pulled back her golden hair and twisted it into a scrunchie on top of her head. Then she grabbed a windbreaker and bolted out the door for coffee with Nina, heading down the hall in long strides.

But she couldn't run from the guilt that was eating away at the pit of her stomach. No matter what Elizabeth did to keep busy, she couldn't avoid coming home to the eerie silence of her dorm room—or knowing that Jessica's absence was all her fault.

What kind of sister am I? she asked herself as she hurried down the stairs to the lobby. How could she stand by and do nothing while Jessica's whole life unraveled? And how could she be avoiding her now instead of standing by her?

But the worst part, the dark core of her guilt, was knowing that in spite of everything that was happening to Jessica, Elizabeth was still thinking about Mike. And hoping he would call.

Jessica was sitting in the shadows of late afternoon, still in her bathrobe, still watching TV on the living-room couch, when she was startled by the doorbell. She sat up bolt upright and stayed stock-still, wondering if she should do something. Then she heard the front door open and her parents' faint voices. "So good to see you. . . . Thanks so much for coming on such short notice. . . ."

Company? Jessica wondered, bewildered. *But I'm not even dressed!*

Mr. and Mrs. Wakefield appeared in the doorway. "Jessica, honey," her mother said, "we want you to meet someone." Her parents filed into the room, followed by a balding man in a white jacket who carried a black briefcase.

"This is Dr. Crawford," her father explained. "He's a"—Mr. Wakefield cleared his throat—"*specialist.* Your old family doctor—remember Dr. Tyler?—recommended him. He's going to ask you some questions. We think he might be able to help you, ah . . . feel better."

Dr. Crawford sat down on the couch beside Jessica, set down his briefcase, and turned on a lamp that sat on an end table. Then he gently extracted the remote control from her hand and clicked off the TV. Jessica's eyes darted to the blank gray screen in mild alarm. Instinctively she hugged her arms protectively to her chest.

"Now, then, Jessica," Dr. Crawford was saying. Up close, with the lights on, she could see that his face was covered with liver spots, and black hair sprouted from his ears. "We're going to play a little game. Won't that be fun?"

Jessica stared blankly at him, then looked

53

worriedly at her parents, who were still standing huddled together by the doorway. They nodded encouragingly.

Dr. Crawford had produced a series of flash cards, each dotted with a bright splash of color, and spread them out on the coffee table. "Now, Jessica," he said. "Let's pretend the colors on these cards symbolize your moods. Can you tell me what color you're feeling now?"

Feeling? Color? Confused, Jessica scanned the array of bright reds, yellows, blues, greens, purples. She could feel everyone's expectant eyes on her. Her gaze hit on a black card. Black was the color of night, when her angel came to her. That was the best feeling she knew of. Tentatively she unfurled her arms and stretched out a shaky finger toward the black card. She glanced up at her parents and read disappointment on their faces. "Is that the wrong answer?" she asked in a small voice.

Dr. Crawford clicked the cap of a ballpoint pen and wrote something down on a pad he had extracted from his briefcase. "There are no right or wrong answers, Jessica," he explained without looking up at her. "Just be honest—that's the only way I'll be able to help you."

"OK," Jessica said, anxiously twisting the belt of her bathrobe in her hands. She hated tests. And this one already seemed to be going badly—she felt as if she'd let her parents down somehow.

"Next game." Dr. Crawford swept up the deck of color cards and took out another stack from his briefcase. "Jessica, I'm going to show you some inkblots. You just tell me what you see in them. You can make up a story or just describe the picture—whatever pops into your head. It's up to you."

Jessica nodded obediently and stared hard at the card he held up. The ink was arranged in two symmetrical, round shapes with a dark oblong between them. It looked just like a body with wings. Jessica frowned. *What did Mom and Dad tell him?* she wondered. Was the doctor trying to trip her up by showing her something that looked so much like an angel?

"Is—is this a trick?" she asked hesitantly.

"A trick?" Dr. Crawford repeated. "What do you mean, a trick?"

"Well . . ." Jessica swallowed hard. "I mean, did you show me a picture of an angel on purpose?"

The doctor raised his eyebrows. "An angel? Please, explain."

"Well, you know, because of my guardian angel," Jessica went on. This time she was sure she had the right answer—she saw through the game. "I thought maybe you showed me that picture to get me to talk about my angel. I mean, what else could it be? There's the body, and there are the wings, and there . . ."

She trailed off, suddenly aware that her mother's face was buried in her father's shoulder and her father was giving her mother comforting pats on the back. Jessica knitted her brows, confused.

Dr. Crawford stared at her for a second, then started writing furiously on his pad. After a second he looked up and flashed Jessica the kind of benevolent smile people gave small children. "Thanks for your time, Jessica," he said briskly. "I think I've heard all I need to hear."

Tom trod lightly down the lush, peach-carpeted hallway of the Theta sorority house. Greek Row was definitely not his scene, but as long as he was asking Lila Fowler a favor, he figured he'd do it on her territory. People of Lila's so-called social standing tended to appreciate a good grovel.

As he approached the drawing room, he could hear Lila's imperious voice carry down the hall. "Come *on*, Bruce. There are a dozen Sigma brothers who would be *lucky* to get a date with Chloe Murphy. You can find *someone* to fix up with her. Somebody must owe you a favor!"

"Lila, you obviously don't understand the guy code of honor," a booming male voice shot back. "A blind date isn't just *a* favor. In the guy world that's like signing an IOU for the rest of your life. No way am I calling in all my chips for one of your random family friends."

Tom peered through the doorway and saw Lila Fowler and her boyfriend, Bruce Patman, sitting across from each other in overstuffed leather armchairs by the fireplace. They were staring each other down with studied concentration, as if there were an invisible chessboard between them. Tom suppressed a smile. Lila and Bruce were both only children from immensely privileged backgrounds, which meant they were perfect for each other—and that they were constantly bickering.

"Come *onnn,* Bruce," Lila whined, sticking out her lower lip. Tom had never seen anyone carry on a conversation while maintaining such a clearly defined pout. "It's just for one night. And she's a *fabulous* catch. Comes from a good family, very sophisticated, great personality . . ."

"Ohhh no, no, no." Bruce waved his hands in the air. "That's like *the* kiss of death for a blind date. In guy-speak 'great personality' is code for 'fell off the ugly tree and didn't miss a branch on the way down.'"

Tom rolled his eyes. *It's macho jerks like Patman who make it harder for the rest of us,* he thought wryly.

Lila's flawless, ivory skin turned a subtle shade of purple. "Of all the obnoxious, offensive—"

Tom cleared his throat and took an uneasy step into the drawing room. "Hey, guys, I hope I'm not interrupting. . . ."

"Oh, hello, Tom," Lila said. "You're not interrupting at all—I'm glad you're here. Maybe you can show my uncouth, oafish lout of a boyfriend the way a *civilized* man behaves."

"Now hang on just a minute—," Bruce protested.

"Anyway," Tom continued, hovering between their chairs, "Lila, I need to talk to you about something. It's about Isabella."

"Just because I don't want to subject one of my frat brothers to a girl who belongs in a kennel doesn't mean I'm uncivilized!" Bruce declared, leaning forward and jabbing a finger at Lila.

"She's a very pretty girl!" Lila insisted. "Besides, it's *one* night. She's only in town for a few days. Come on, Bruce—it would be so rude to make her tag along with us like a third wheel!"

"As I was saying," Tom continued with a little cough, "I'm sure you know Isabella's parents took her to a hospital in Switzerland. But they didn't tell Danny where. And, um . . . he's not taking it so well. He really misses her."

"Funny." Lila sniffed and patted her perfect brunette bun. "I keep forgetting that *some* men actually have hearts. Unlike *this* unfeeling lunkhead." She jerked her thumb toward Bruce in a most un-Fowler-like gesture.

"Well, if I'm such a lunkhead, I'm sure one of *my* friends wouldn't be good enough for *your* friend anyway," Bruce retorted. "You can find another sucker to fix up with Crusty."

"*Chloe!*" Lila screeched.

Bruce threw up his hands. "Whatever."

Tom was running out of patience. He took a deep breath. "Lila, please. I obviously came at a bad time, but I swear I'll be out of your hair in a minute if you could just help me out." Tom laced his hands together beseechingly. "I'm begging you, if you know *anything* about where Isabella went, *please* tell me. I've got to get in touch with her for Danny's sake. *Please,* Lila, I'll do anything."

Lila slowly turned her head and regarded Tom with new interest, as if something had just occurred to her. "Anything, huh?" A catlike smile stretched across her face. "You know, Tom, you're not a bad-looking guy. I bet you clean up pretty well."

Tom gulped. He had a feeling he knew where this was going.

"I can make a couple of calls and find out what hospital Isabella's staying at," Lila continued, putting a thoughtful finger to her lips. "*If* you do something for me. Chloe Murphy, the *lovely* daughter of family friends, is coming into town next week, and Bruce and I need someone to double with us."

"Hey, Watts, she's got a great personality," Bruce mimicked, snickering. "*Sucker!*"

Lila shot Bruce a death look and turned back to Tom. "So, are you on board?"

Tom hesitated. He was ashamed to admit that he shared some of Bruce's reservations about blind dates—Tom hated to sympathize with a chauvinist like Patman. *Well, Danny's happiness is at stake,* he reasoned. "Yeah, I'm in," he said finally. After all, it was just for one night. How bad could it be?

"So I'm going to start her out at this dosage," Dr. Crawford said, handing a piece of paper to Mr. Wakefield. "I'll have my office schedule a follow-up appointment in a few weeks, and we can talk about adjusting the prescription if she seems to be doing better."

Jessica sat curled up on the couch, clutching a sofa pillow tightly against her chest. She was trying to concentrate on a soap opera that used to be one of her favorites, but she couldn't blot out the doctor's voice. He was standing just a few feet away, talking to her parents as if she weren't even in the room.

At the edge of her vision she saw her father look dubiously at the piece of paper Dr. Crawford had given him. "Three a day?" Ned Wakefield asked doubtfully. "Isn't that a rather large dosage?"

Dr. Crawford waved dismissively. "It's a mild sedative. Based on what you've told me about her recent history, Jessica's condition is probably stress related. And what she needs right now is pure, undisturbed rest. That's what's going to get her out of the woods."

Sedatives? The back of Jessica's neck prickled. *They're going to drug me?* She hugged the cushion tighter. She wanted to ask a million questions, but the doctor seemed scary and aloof. And her parents were staring at her with strangely resigned concern. Jessica didn't want to worry them any further.

"Thank you, Doctor," Mr. Wakefield said finally. "We'll get this filled in the morning."

Dr. Crawford produced a small vial. "I brought a couple of samples. She can start with these."

Jessica burrowed her chin into the pillow. She couldn't understand why her parents wanted to put her on drugs or why everyone was treating her like a little baby who couldn't think for herself. But if they wanted her to take pills, she would take them. If they were bad for her, her guardian angel would find a way to tell her. He wouldn't let anything bad happen to her.

_____

"So then I told Bryan I *wasn't* threatened by the fact that he happens to have an attractive, young, female TA—but if there was some reason I *should* be, he'd damn well better let me know about it." Nina Harper snorted vehemently. "And do you know what that dog said to me? *Do* you?"

Nina let out an exasperated sigh and waved her biscotti in front of Elizabeth's face like a wand. "Liz, are you listening to a word I'm saying? Your eyes are as glazed over as that pastry you're not eating."

"What? Oh." Startled, Elizabeth looked down at the apple Danish that lay on a plate before her. She and Nina were seated at a terrace table at Tea and Sympathy, a cozy café off campus. But nothing, not Nina's company, the jazz softly piping through the outdoor speakers, or the extra cocoa shavings in her Mochaccino, had soothed Elizabeth's jangled

63

nerves. All she could think about was having to go back to her barren, empty room alone. And what would she do if Jessica called back?

"I'm sorry, Nina; I'm just a little distracted," Elizabeth said sheepishly. "I've been under a lot of stress lately." She picked up her Danish and took a bite.

"Oh, I'm just giving you a hard time, Liz." Nina grinned warmly. "I'm sorry I've been babbling on about my dumb boyfriend. Tell me how you're doing. How is it with Jess being gone?"

"Well," Elizabeth said, straining to keep her voice light, "it sure is easier to get work done without the one-woman tornado around—I'll say that much." She let out a forced little laugh from somewhere in the back of her throat.

Nina raised her eyebrows. She lifted her mug of espresso to her lips and eyed Elizabeth as if she were trying to scope out what her friend was really thinking. Elizabeth focused her attention on her Danish, willing Nina to understand that it was just too painful to talk about Jessica right now.

"That *is* a plus," Nina agreed finally, sounding as if she'd decided to play along. "My roommate is always either blasting hard-core punk music or talking on the phone to her weird friends—or both. I have to flee to the library just to hear myself think."

An idea seized Elizabeth. She set her Danish back down on the plate and leaned across the table eagerly. "Hey, Nina, you could stay in my room if you wanted! I mean, you know I'm an even bigger nerd than you, so I wouldn't distract you." Elizabeth grinned. "We'd get obscene amounts of work done. What do you say?"

Nina laughed. "Nah, that's OK, Liz. It's not that big a deal. Besides, I don't want to impose on you."

"Oh, you wouldn't be imposing at all!" Elizabeth insisted, hearing the unnaturally high note in her own voice. "It would be fun! I mean, don't you think we'd make good roommates?" Elizabeth squeezed her cappuccino mug anxiously between her fingertips. It suddenly seemed vitally important that Nina stay with her. Now that she'd thought of having her best friend keep her company, the idea of returning to the cavernous emptiness of the dorm room seemed unbearable.

Nina hesitated, again looking as if she were trying to size up Elizabeth's real feelings. "Sure, but I bet you want your privacy—"

"No, I *don't*," Elizabeth said, a little louder and more forcefully than she intended. "I'd love the company."

A huge part of Elizabeth wanted to spill her guts to her best friend, to beg Nina outright to be there for her. But that would mean confessing just how shaken she was by Jessica's condition, and Elizabeth wasn't ready to do that. "*Please*, Nina," she added in a low voice.

At last Nina nodded slowly. "OK, Liz, thanks." Her tone made it obvious that she knew she was doing Elizabeth a favor, not the other way around. "I'd be happy to stay with you. You know you can always count on me. And once we're around each other all the time, maybe you'll feel comfortable enough to tell me how you *really* feel about Jessica being gone."

"Wyatt's open on the three-point line. He gets the ball. He's going for the three! He shoots. He scores!"

Danny whooped as the basketball he'd lofted into the air sank neatly into the wastebasket in the corner. Scoring three points off the Lakers, even the *imaginary* Lakers, was the most exciting thing that had happened to him all night.

Tom, hunched over his desk, craned his head around to glare at Danny. "Yo, I'm happy to know you have a healthy, active fantasy life, but could you keep it down? I have fifty pages of modern-European-history reading to finish for tomorrow."

"Sorry," Danny said, getting up to fish the basketball out of the wastebasket. "I'm just bored. I don't feel like doing any work, and there's nothing else to do."

"Well, there's plenty of nothing going on all over campus, in places where people *aren't* trying to study," Tom said grumpily.

Danny rolled his eyes and made a face.

"Excuse me, Mr. Delicate Genius. Fine, I'll entertain myself."

He looked at his watch. Seven-thirty—he could still catch happy hour at Farrell's Tavern if he hurried.

No bars, he told himself sternly. *No booze tonight. There's plenty of fun stuff to do around campus without getting wasted—and without Isabella.*

He just couldn't remember any of that stuff at the moment.

Danny dribbled the ball idly against the floor. *Think, Wyatt,* he commanded himself. *What did I do with myself before Isabella came into the picture?* The pathetic truth was, he'd been part of a couple for so long, he couldn't remember how he used to spend his time as a single guy. That is, other than chasing girls—and Danny most definitely did *not* want to seek contact with the opposite sex right now. He'd suffered enough already.

Guy stuff, Danny thought. But what did guys do together anyway . . . other than drink and chase girls?

"Hey, Tombo," Danny said impulsively as he landed another perfect wastebasket field goal. "I was thinking of rounding up a bunch of guys, shooting some hoops. Just a pickup game—nothing too high stress."

Tom craned his head and looked at Danny incredulously. "Right now?"

"No, but . . . soon," Danny decided. "I need time to get everybody together. You in?"

"Sure, man, I'll be there." Tom turned back to his textbook.

Feeling pleased with himself, Danny picked up the phone to call some guys from Sigma. Basketball—that was a perfect guy thing. Not too much talking, not too much thinking—and most important, no drinking.

See, there's plenty to do without Isabella, Danny assured himself. *Fun stuff*—healthy *stuff*. All of a sudden he felt as if he had taken his first step to putting his life back together . . . his life as a free agent, without Isabella.

Jessica was floating . . . no, flying. She was still in her bed, but at the same time she could see her bed beneath her and her body on top of it. Her golden hair was fanned out around her face on the pillow, her eyes peacefully closed. Jessica could see that her sleeping face wore a tranquil smile. *She must be having a nice dream,* Jessica thought affectionately.

Suddenly, across the dark, muddled fog of the air, a soft voice echoed. At first it was formless, indistinct, like a sound traveling underwater. Then . . .

"Jessica!"

That voice . . . so familiar . . . *No, it couldn't be,* Jessica's floating self told her sleeping self. *You're dreaming.*

"Jeeesss . . . iii . . . caaa!"

His voice was the most achingly beautiful sound she had ever heard. It beckoned her, like a siren song. The whole room seemed to quiver and shimmer with the rhythm of those sweet syllables. Irresistibly drawn, Jessica stretched out her ghostly pale arms, propelling herself across the room.

She floated over to the window, and—as she'd known in her heart she would—saw her angel through the pane. It looked as if he were floating in midair.

Awed tears sprang to Jessica's eyes. For the first time she could make out his face, crystal clear. It was breathtakingly handsome. It was divinely gorgeous. It was . . .

"Nick?" Jessica whispered. "Nick, is it really you?"

Frantically she opened the window without tearing her eyes from his face. It had to be him. Every feature was Nick's, down to the bottomless brown eyes that searched hers with distraught grief.

But wait—Nick's eyes are green! Jessica thought confusedly. It was Nick, and yet his stubble-covered face was . . . different somehow.

"Jessica, my poor, sweet Jessica," he was murmuring, his voice low and urgent. "What's happened to you?" It was Nick's voice; there was no doubt in her mind. She could place it now.

"But I thought you were . . . ," she began tremulously, then trailed off, dizzy. Everything was spinning. But Nick's angel face shone bright and vivid, silver in the moonlight. It had to be a dream. . . .

But it seems so real! How could I just be imagining Nick? Jessica's mind was reeling. If only she wasn't so drowsy . . . if only her head wasn't so thick and sleep addled . . .

"Oh, baby, what have they done to you?" Nick's voice was mournful. "Don't give up, Jessica . . . don't give up. . . ."

Jessica wanted desperately to answer him, but when she opened her mouth, no sound came out. Against her will her eyes were fluttering shut, blurring the image of Nick's face into an indistinct shower of sparks. Then her knees seemed to melt into folds of silk and billow out underneath her. Jessica felt the cool, flat floor against her cheek, and everything went black.

"Liz, are you there? Are you there? Are you there, Liz? It's me, Jess!"

There was a long pause that crackled with static. Elizabeth stood over her answering machine, hugging her arms to her chest.

"Well, OK, I guess . . . I guess you're not there." Jessica's tinny, plaintive voice dropped to a trembling whisper, made even more warbly by the tape. "I'm going to bed now, but please, please,

please call me back soon, Liz. I need to tell you what the TV said about my ange—"

Elizabeth stabbed at the stop button on the machine. She turned and cringed to see Nina sitting on Jessica's bed, staring pityingly at her.

"I guess she called when I was in the shower," Nina said almost apologetically. "Liz, Jess sounds like she's not doing too well. Do you want to talk about it at all?"

Elizabeth took off her jacket and draped it on her desk chair, turning her back to Nina. "No, it's fine. You know Jessica—she can take care of herself." She felt a twinge of guilt as she uttered the words . . . but she was afraid that if she admitted the truth, she wouldn't be able to hold back the flood of emotions inside her.

"Are you sure, Liz? You looked pretty upset."

It was annoying sometimes how well Nina knew her. "Oh . . . well . . . actually," Elizabeth said, keeping her voice even, "I was just kind of disappointed. When you said I had a message, I thought . . . well, I was hoping it was from this guy I'm kind of seeing."

The distraction tactic worked. Nina's narrowed eyes opened wide in surprise. "You have a new man? When did this happen? Who *is* he?"

Elizabeth flushed. "His name is . . . Mike." She chose not to mention that it was actually *Mike McAllery,* her sister's ex-husband. There was no telling how Nina would take that news . . .

especially since Elizabeth wasn't sure how she felt about it herself.

"Mike, huh? So spill!" Nina exclaimed eagerly. "How did you meet him? What year is he?"

"Actually, he doesn't go to school," Elizabeth said carefully. "He works on cars. We met when I took the Jeep in to be fixed." *That's* sort of *true*, Elizabeth conceded guiltily to herself. She'd run into Mike at the body shop after the twins' Jeep broke down, and their relationship had developed from there.

"A mechanic, huh?" Nina grinned wickedly. "I guess he's good with his hands."

Elizabeth's face was burning. "I guess you could say that," she admitted, lacing her fingers nervously in her lap. "But—but—well, there's more to our relationship than *that*."

"Details," Nina ordered. "Since Bryan and I haven't done anything romantic in weeks, I'll have to live vicariously through you. So what do you guys do together? Dinner? Dancing?"

What do *we do when we're together?* Elizabeth hesitated, racking her brain. They'd never gone dancing, and the last time they went out to eat, they just ended up making out in the parking lot.

"Oh yeah, yeah—all that stuff," Elizabeth finally said breezily. "We have a lot in common." *Actually, I hardly know anything about him,* she realized. When was the last time she asked him about his work restoring cars . . . or he asked her about school? The only thing she and Mike definitely shared was their attraction for each other—and their concern for Jessica.

"That sounds great, Liz." Nina got up and went over to hug Elizabeth. "With everything that's going on in your life, I'm really glad you met somebody nice."

"Thanks, Nina." Elizabeth smiled weakly. Inside, she was on fire with shame. What kind of relationship was she involved in that she had to tell her best friend lies and half-truths about it?

A purely physical relationship, that's what kind, Elizabeth admitted to herself. And it wasn't even much of one at that . . . as long as she wasn't willing to go too far.

Golden morning sunlight streamed through Jessica's bedroom. Jessica snuggled under the covers and burrowed her cheek against the soft hollow of her pillows, a blissful smile on her face.

"I won't give up, Nick," she murmured happily into her pillow. "I know you're watching out for me."

In spite of the warm blankets gathered around her shoulders, Jessica shivered in her sleep. A cool breeze gently brushed her face. Jessica's heavy-lidded eyes blinked open. After a second they shut again. She wriggled deeper under the blankets, the thick mantle of sleep again sinking over her.

Suddenly the back of her neck prickled.

Consciousness hit her like a bucket of ice water. A breeze was blowing . . . but how could that be? The window had definitely been closed when she went to sleep!

Jessica sat bolt upright in bed, threw off the covers, and bounded to the window. Sure enough, it was wide open. The cool air gently rustled her white curtains; the gauzy fabric rippled toward her like ghostly, grasping hands.

All at once her dream came rushing back to her, as real and solid as the cold wooden floorboards under her bare feet. "My angel!" Jessica cried, tears of shocked joy springing to her eyes. "He was really here! It was *real!*"

Eagerly she craned her head out the window, hoping against hope to see some trace of him . . . maybe some fairy dust, like in the stories she'd read as a little girl. But there was nothing.

Overcome, Jessica ducked back inside and sank onto the floor, drawing her knees up to her chest. She was shaking all over.

It had to be real, she told herself, wrapping her arms around her legs. *He was here . . . the angel . . . Nick! It had to be him—I saw his face!* She was rocking back and forth now in a desperate attempt to comfort herself. *It seemed so real! I* couldn't *have dreamed it!*

Chapter Six

"OK, mission accomplished. I called my contacts, and I got the info."

It took Tom a second to place the imperiously breezy voice on the other end of the line. "Hello to you too, Lila. Hang on—let me get a pen." He wedged the phone receiver into the crook of his neck and rummaged through the papers strewn across the surface of his dorm-room desk. "OK, shoot."

"Mr. and Mrs. Ricci took Isabella to L'Institut Duchamp," Lila explained in a crisp, matter-of-fact tone. "It's an in-patient therapy facility for people with severe neurological disorders."

Tom wrote down the address and phone number she read him. "Thanks, Lila. I really appreciate this."

"No problem." Lila's voice softened. "Good luck getting in touch with her, Tom. Izzy's one of my best friends—I'm worried about her too."

Tom couldn't help smiling. "Lila Fowler, you big softie."

"Yes. Well." Lila cleared her throat, her usual supercilious tone returning. "Now, about what *you* can do for *me*. I hope you didn't think I forgot about our little bargain."

Tom rolled his eyes to the ceiling. He was definitely not thrilled about the prospect of spending an evening with Lila and Bruce and one of Lila's snobby, prissy friends. "A deal's a deal—just tell me what to do."

"Well, I'll have to call you back with the exact details, but leave your nights free early next week," Lila said. "Chloe was going to come in this weekend, but she decided to visit another college first."

Tom's jaw dropped open. "Did you just say *visit* a college, as in, what people do when they're *applying* to college?" he asked apprehensively.

"Why, yes, Chloe is a high-school senior." Tom could practically hear Lila's smirk over the phone. "Didn't I mention that to you?"

Tom exhaled in exasperation. "No, Lila, you certainly didn't." This was all he needed. On top of being part of Lila's super-privileged circle, this Chloe was an immature high-school girl. Now he was stuck entertaining some spoiled little princess. Tom groaned. What had he gotten himself into?

*   *   *

"OK, don't move a muscle," Todd commanded. "This requires complete concentration."

Obediently Dana lay still on the grassy quad, her head tilted back, her lips parted. The afternoon sunlight glinted off the dark waves of her hair. Admiring the exquisite arc of her throat, Todd reached into the bag of popcorn he was holding and lobbed one of the kernels at Dana. It missed her open mouth by a mile, instead landing on her forehead.

Dana exploded into peals of laughter, her shoulders lifting off the ground. "And you used to be a hotshot basketball star?" she teased, her hazel eyes twinkling. "At this rate I'll starve to death!"

"No, really, I can do this," Todd insisted. He was bent over laughing. It was so much fun to be with someone he could act silly around. "I swear—c'mon, hold still. And stop making me laugh!"

Dana rolled her eyes in exaggerated impatience and opened her mouth again. Todd aimed another kernel of popcorn. This time it landed squarely in her mouth.

"Good shot, Wilkins!" Dana exclaimed when she was done crunching. She sat up and wrapped her long, lithe arms around his neck, tousling his hair with her fingers. "For that you deserve a kiss," she added in a lower voice as she leaned toward him.

As Dana's soft lips pressed against his, Todd

pulled her closer. In a second he was lost in her kiss, only dimly aware of the bustle of students crossing the quad on their way to class. Todd had never really been into major PDAs, but right now he didn't feel the least bit embarrassed. Dana was talented and funny and beautiful—she looked especially cute today in her shoulder-baring, red, retro flowered sundress and chunky white clogs. Any guy would be lucky to have her, and Todd felt proud to let the world know she was all his. When they pulled apart, he felt like shouting at the top of his lungs, *I love Dana Upshaw!*

"Mmmm," Dana murmured dreamily, her dark lashes fluttering. "That was amazing . . . but weren't we supposed to be studying?" She disentangled a hand from his hair and gestured toward the untouched pile of books beside them on the grass.

"Oh, *that.*" Todd grinned. A couple of his buddies from his basketball days walked by, and Todd raised his hand in salutation as they passed. "I've always thought studying was overrated anyway."

"But—," Dana protested. Todd ducked his head quickly forward and silenced her with a kiss. Then he laced his fingers around Dana's waist and tipped backward, pulling Dana down onto the grass on top of him.

She squealed with laughter as they rolled together on the quad, finally landing in one tangled sprawl of limbs. "Todd, you're insane!"

Todd chuckled as he gazed up at Dana's lovely, flushed face, hovering over him. "No, just madly in love," he said, reaching up to tuck a lock of hair behind her ear.

The next time he looked up, he saw Nina Harper and Bryan Nelson coming down the steps of the library. Todd gave them a friendly wave, then turned back to Dana and saw her gazing intently at him. *Can she tell how proud I am to be seen with her?* Todd wondered hopefully. More than anything he wanted Dana to trust him, to know he was in it for the long haul.

"So," Todd said, waggling his eyebrows, "as long as you're on top of me, I was thinking . . ."

"Nice try, Wilkins." Dana rolled off him and punched him playfully on the shoulder.

"OK, OK." Todd grinned sheepishly, putting up his hands in surrender. "You can't blame a guy for trying." *Especially when his hormones are in overdrive,* he added to himself. As happy as he was with Dana now, Todd was more than ready to take the next step in their relationship.

But I don't want to screw this up, he reminded himself, gazing ardently into Dana's eyes. He'd wait as long as it took for Dana to trust him one hundred percent.

Jessica idly pushed her toothbrush around in her mouth, staring into the eyes of her mirror image. It was strange not to see Elizabeth's reflection next to her own or Elizabeth herself out of the corner of her eye. Without Elizabeth, Jessica was incomplete. She knew the girl in the mirror was herself, but it was as if she were staring into the face of a stranger.

Funny—back in high school, she and her twin used to fight constantly over bathroom time. But now Jessica would have given anything to have Elizabeth here with her.

Jessica's eyes filled with tears. "Liz, what can I do to bring you back?" she murmured. The bathroom felt so empty, so barren without any traces of her sister. Even the towel racks on Elizabeth's side of the bathroom looked naked.

That's it! A jolt of energy pierced Jessica. Hastily she rinsed out her mouth, then ran into Elizabeth's bedroom and rummaged through the closet. She found what she was looking for—the ratty, threadbare sky blue terry-cloth bathrobe that Elizabeth had worn throughout high school—and raced back into the bathroom. She hung the bathrobe triumphantly on the back of Elizabeth's door and stepped back to admire her handiwork. A warm, comforting feeling of nostalgia tingled through her limbs.

"Wait, I know." Jessica hurried down the hall to the linen closet and returned with an armful of Elizabeth's favorite towels—the pale yellow ones with the sunflower pattern. Lovingly, Jessica looped the towels over their hooks. Then she grabbed a bottle of her lotion, a brand that Elizabeth sometimes used, and placed it carefully on Elizabeth's side of the counter. Jessica couldn't remember the last time she'd been so excited. With all Elizabeth's things arranged just so, Jessica half expected her sister to walk into the bathroom any minute. And when Elizabeth came home and saw how she made everything all nice for her, maybe she'd want to stay. They'd be together, like old times!

Her loneliness fading by the second, Jessica racked her brain for other ways she could make her twin feel more at home. "I know!" She clapped. "Liz likes everything clean—she's always yelling at me for being so messy." Crouching, she opened the cabinet under the bathroom sink and pulled out several cleaning products and some sponges.

"Wait'll you see how clean it is, Liz," Jessica muttered intently under her breath, sprinkling a thick dusting of cleanser across Elizabeth's side of the counter. Bearing down hard with her sponge, she scrubbed the counter in long, furious strokes. "You'll see—I'll make everything just the way you like it. . . . It'll be *just* like the old days!"

Jessica was abuzz with enthusiasm. She scoured circles on the tile, humming happily to herself. Then her elbow knocked against something. She whirled to see a bottle of oil soap explode on the floor, an oozing, amber puddle spreading on the white tile.

"No!" Jessica gasped, dropping to her knees. "No, stop—*stop!*" She tried cupping the sticky liquid in her hands, but it dripped through her fingers. She reached wildly for a sponge, but each frantic stroke made the oily brown surface bubble up into an ever widening pool.

"No, stay *clean!*" Jessica panted hysterically. "Liz likes everything *clean!*" Stringy locks of her blond hair were trailing in the grimy puddle, oil stains darkening on the knees of her pajamas.

Tears of frustration and panic pricked her eyes. Everything had gone so wrong! Elizabeth would never want to come home now that she'd made such a mess—never!

Jessica felt filthy all over, caked in the slimy grease. The harder she rubbed, the more sickeningly dirty she became. "I'm so dirty and disgusting!" she cried. "I would make Liz *sick* if she saw me!"

Jessica's hand slipped on the waxy tile, and she fell hard on her side onto the floor. She curled up into a ball and lay sobbing.

The awful, acrid-smelling oil soap was still spreading inexorably across the floor, seeping into every fiber of her pajamas and every pore of her skin. But she had no strength to rise. Only one terrified thought bubbled up from the streaked floor.

What if Liz never comes back?

"Listen, Isabella," Tom said awkwardly, "Danny needs you. Please, just talk to him, one last time."

No, that sounded goofy, Tom decided as his words echoed across the walls of his dorm room. He sat at his desk, fingering the slip of paper where he had written down both the address and the main number for L'Institut Duchamp. *Think, Watts! This is Danny's life at stake— you don't want to sound like a dweeb.*

He considered the possibility that Isabella might not even answer the phone. Tom cleared his throat and tried again. "Mr. and Mrs. Ricci, you know your daughter cared for Danny very deeply. Don't you think you owe it to her . . ."

Scratch that, he decided, trailing off. He could already hear the response in his mind: *Tom who? Who the heck are you to tell us what we owe our daughter?*

Tom sighed and pushed back his desk chair. He got up and started pacing the room. Maybe a letter would be best—that would give Isabella some time to think. But what if her parents never even showed her the letter? Worse, what if they returned it unopened and Danny found it? He'd probably be furious with Tom for meddling behind his back.

And he'd have every right to be, Tom conceded. *If it were Danny approaching Elizabeth on my behalf, I know I'd want to kill him.* He picked up the picture frame that was lying facedown on Danny's nightstand and stared at the photo inside. It was a snapshot of Danny and Isabella in happier days, which Danny had turned over soon after she left. "I'm never going to see her again, so why should I remember what she looks like?" Danny had snarled bitterly. And yet he'd left the frame there, facedown though it was.

The more he thought about it, the more Tom was convinced that contacting Isabella without Danny's permission was a big mistake. He replaced the frame on the nightstand. As much as he wanted to help his buddy, it just wasn't his place to interfere.

Tom folded up the slip of paper and tucked it into the pocket of his navy, crew-neck T-shirt. *It's Danny's call,* he decided. Tom would pass along the phone number, and from then on it would be in Danny's hands.

"Fine, don't do me any favors," Nina snapped into the phone. "I'll find someone else to go to the stupid movie with me!" She slammed down the receiver and made an infuriated huffing noise.

Elizabeth craned her head around in her desk chair and gave Nina a wryly sympathetic smile. "Trouble in paradise?" she asked.

"*That's* an understatement," Nina growled. "I mean, it's not that I don't respect Bryan's dedication. But I can't believe there's not one single other person in the entire Black Student Union who could put up some dumb flyers so Bryan could make time to go out with me."

"It does seem like he could work around it if he wanted to," Elizabeth agreed.

Nina buried her face in her hands and groaned. "Ever since I pointed out that this Maria Laurence was spending more time with him than any TA's spent on a student in the history of academia, it's like he's been going out of his way to test my trust. Am I doing something wrong, or is it just that men are scum?"

Elizabeth got up and went to sit by Nina on the bed. "Right now, I'd have to pick option *B*," she said, slinging a comforting arm across Nina's shoulders. "Look at *my* track record—Tom Watts, whom I *thought* was the love of my life, believes I'm an evil, frigid ice princess." She shook her head, still smarting at the memory of Tom's words. "And Mike appears to have dropped off the face of the earth."

Nina lifted her head and gave Elizabeth a commiserating half smile. "He still hasn't called, huh?"

"Nope," Elizabeth confirmed, more lightly than she felt. As confusing as her relationship with Mike was, it was torture being left in the dark. "I don't think he wants anything to do with me. I just wish he would come out and say it."

"Awww, I'm sorry, Liz," Nina said earnestly. "But hey, if it wasn't meant to be, better you found out sooner than later. You'll meet another guy."

"I guess." Elizabeth looked down at Nina's patchwork bedspread, suddenly wishing she'd never opened the can of worms named Mike. She met Nina's eyes and grinned wickedly. "Well, I could always give Todd a call," she pointed out, lightly jabbing Nina's ribs with her elbow. "It didn't work out our first couple of tries, but maybe the third time's the charm."

Nina laughed, but it was a short, strained little bark of a laugh. Then she averted her eyes, as if she had found an extremely interesting piece of lint on her jeans.

Elizabeth frowned. "Nina, what is it?"

"What? Oh. Nothing," Nina said with forced-sounding lightness, not looking up.

"Nina, I know you too well!" Elizabeth folded her arms across her chest. "Something is up—now, out with it!"

Nina sighed. "OK, Liz. It's just that . . . I saw Todd on the quad today, and he was . . . well, let's just say it looks like he's off the market." She looked apologetically at Elizabeth.

"Oh, is that all?" Elizabeth exclaimed, relieved. "Jeez, Nina, it's not like I was serious about getting back with him. In fact, I'm happy for him. So who is it—anyone I know?"

Nina gulped. "See, that's the thing, Liz. It's . . . Dana."

Elizabeth felt as if she had been punched in the gut, the wind knocked out of her. It took a second for her to regain enough breath to gasp, "Dana *Upshaw?*"

Memories flooded back to her as she uttered the name—Tom flaunting Dana all over campus, throwing their relationship in Elizabeth's face; Elizabeth finding the half-empty box of condoms under Tom's bed, knowing he certainly hadn't used them with *her.* . . .

Nina nodded, her round eyes full of worry. "I'm sorry you had to find out like this, Liz. But try not to take it too personally. I mean, a minute ago you were happy Todd found someone. So what if it's Dana that he's happy with?"

Elizabeth snorted in disgust. "*Please.* She just *happened* to go after *another* one of my exes? Obviously she's just doing this to get back at me for Tom!"

Nina opened her mouth as if she were about to say something, then clamped it shut.

"I just can't believe Todd would fall for it," Elizabeth went on, her blood boiling as the words tumbled out in a rush. "I mean, does he really think that Dana is anything other than a conniving, backstabbing little vixen?" Elizabeth felt sick to her stomach. Her relationship with Todd had long since run its course, but she'd believed that they would always remain good friends—and good friends were nothing if not loyal. She shook her head bitterly. "I just don't understand, Nina. How could he betray me like this?"

The Wakefield house cast a long, broad shadow across the moonlit yard. The well-manicured lawn, bright and green and picturesque in the daylight, seemed vaguely sinister at night—ominous somehow. Even to him . . . and he'd known more than his share of fear, of horror.

Under cover of darkness, he crept slowly across the grass. When he reached a tree toward the center of the Wakefields' property, he took the chance to stretch his aching knees and draw himself up to his full six-foot-plus height. A light wind ruffled the tree's branches, and he shivered, his clothes damp from the grass.

I'll be glad when this is over—when I can stop living in the shadows, he reflected. But he wasn't going anywhere until he got to Jessica. Maybe she didn't understand it yet . . . but she was living her life under a shadow too.

Soon, though, all that would change. If he had his way, Jessica would never know suffering like this again.

As if she heard him or felt his presence, Jessica suddenly appeared like a beacon in the square of white light that was her window. Even in the darkness, even from a distance, she was achingly beautiful. Every inch of her face, every dimple, every strand of her golden hair was etched irrevocably in his memory, for him to cherish once she was gone to him forever. Even now he could scarcely believe they would soon be parted for good. *But I have to do what I have to do,* he reminded himself. *For Jessica's sake—and my own.*

Jessica stood motionless in the window, as if she were waiting for something—or someone. He longed to reveal himself to her, but he was afraid she would cry out again. Last time her parents hadn't taken her seriously, hadn't even bothered to go outside and investigate. But they would definitely start getting suspicious if Jessica claimed to see him again. He was skating on thin ice.

After several minutes Jessica's shoulders sank. She turned away from the window and disappeared from view. A moment later the light went out. He waited just long enough to give her time to drift off, then started inching forward.

Just then the kitchen light went on. He backed hastily behind the tree and peered out to see Mr. Wakefield walking across the window.

He swore under his breath. He was so frustrated. He desperately needed to reach Jessica before it was too late. But he could never get close enough in time.

He flattened his back against the tree and exhaled deeply. *Jessica,* he telegraphed silently, *I promise it won't be long. Somehow I'll figure out how to get you alone.*

Chapter Seven

"Hey, look over there," Todd said, stopping suddenly in his tracks and pointing toward a spot in the distance.

"Wha . . ." Dana turned her head, and Todd planted a quick kiss on her lips. He grinned smugly at her, slipping his hand through hers as they resumed walking across campus.

"Hey, no fair!" Dana protested, shoving his chest lightly. "You stole that kiss without asking. I won't stand for that!"

"Oh yeah? What are you going to do about it?" Todd reached around her waist and tickled her ribs.

"I'll have to take it back," Dana asserted, pulling Todd in close.

Todd felt the electric charge between their bodies as Dana's lips parted on his. He ran his hands down her silk-blouse-clad back, inhaling the sweet scent of her perfume—fruity with a hint of jasmine. Playful and sensual, just like Dana herself. Being close to her was intoxicating. He had to force himself to break out of the kiss.

"We've really got to get over this nauseating young-love stage," Dana declared solemnly as they fell into step together again, swinging their tightly laced hands. "I'm sure anyone around us would be appalled."

"Well, then, it's a good thing I don't want to share you with anyone else," Todd said, leaning over to plant a tender kiss on her smooth forehead. "I like being alone with you—just us."

"I do too." Dana tilted her face toward Todd's, her hazel eyes twinkling. "In fact, I'm starting to think we might be able to arrange some quality time alone soon."

"Quality time?" Todd repeated. "Are we talking about, like, playing Parcheesi? Building model planes?"

Dana shrugged and lowered her lashes coyly. "Let's just say I have a good feeling about how things are going between us."

Todd felt his chest expand with excitement. "You just say the word," he urged in a low voice. "Because I would really love to . . . play Parcheesi with you." Grinning, he squeezed her hand in his. "Or, you know, whatever you feel like doing."

Two patches of pink appeared above Dana's cheekbones and spread rapidly across her face. "Listen, Todd, I'm not going to beat around the bush," she said. "The campus pharmacy's up ahead, and I'd like to know I'm prepared in case . . . the mood strikes us." She held up a warning finger before Todd could respond. "But I'm not making any promises, Wilkins. The expiration dates on condoms are usually a couple of years away."

"Ah, I could wait a couple of years, no problem," Todd said lightly as they approached the pharmacy. "As long as I'm with you, they'll fly by." He wished that feeble lie were true . . . but just having this conversation, Todd felt as if he might die of acute hormonal shock.

Dana rolled her eyes. "Very convincing, Sir Laurence Olivier." She gave him a quick kiss on the cheek. "OK, you better wait out here, or you'll make me giggle."

She disappeared into the pharmacy. Obediently Todd stood by the entrance with his hands shoved in his pockets, feeling like a gawky fourteen-year-old as he shifted his weight from foot to foot. As hard as he tried not to get his hopes up, Todd couldn't squelch the stupid little smile that was tugging at the corners of his lips.

He was lost in not altogether wholesome thoughts about Dana as the between-class crunch of students streamed past him. Todd was wondering whether it would be premature to invite Dana up to his room after dinner when he felt a tap on his shoulder.

He spun around and saw Elizabeth Wakefield

standing in front of him. "Liz! What's up?"

"I was just on my way to the *Gazette* office to go over some galleys," Elizabeth said, her expression impassive. "So what are you, ah, up to?" She arched her eyebrows quizzically.

"Actually, I was waiting for my girlfriend," Todd said, his little smile stretching into a broad grin. It was the first time he had used the word *girlfriend* out loud, and it felt good—it felt *right*. He couldn't wait to tell Elizabeth all about his feelings for Dana. Elizabeth was one of his oldest friends; she would be thrilled to hear that he was in love again.

"So even though we really haven't been together all that long, I feel like I've known her all my life," Todd was saying, a sickeningly sappy look in his eyes. "I can't remember the last time I was this happy."

Elizabeth wondered if her face was turning purple. She couldn't believe Todd had actually admitted that he was seeing Dana Upshaw, much less that he had regaled her with a gushy monologue detailing all the reasons why Dana was the most wonderful person on earth. *And that goofy grin on his face is really too much to bear,* she noted in annoyance.

Unbelievably, Todd was still talking. "So I want to take her out for a big, romantic eve—"

"Listen, Todd," Elizabeth cut in, more sharply

than she had intended. "There's something I need to talk to you about."

Todd looked wary. "OK, go for it."

Elizabeth took a deep breath. How could she put this diplomatically? "It's about Dana. I just think you should be . . . careful."

Todd's brows creased. "Liz, I know you have kind of a weird history with Dana, but she's really changed," he said in a hurt voice. "She feels really bad about how immature she acted with Tom."

Stealing the apology letter Tom wrote me when we were broken up was more than just immature *in my book—it was positively evil,* Elizabeth wanted to say. Instead she said in a patient voice, "Todd, she may *say* she's changed, but you said yourself you don't know her that well. All I'm saying is, just take things slow. Keep your guard up."

"Keep my *guard* up? What kind of thing is that to say?" Todd sounded really indignant now. "Liz, you're my friend. And you know how down I've been since Gin-Yung died. Can't you just be happy for me?"

Frustration coiled inside Elizabeth's stomach. "I'm telling you this because I *want* you to be happy, Todd! I don't trust Dana, and I don't want to see you get hurt!"

Todd's brown eyes clouded over. "You know, Elizabeth, you really should learn to keep your opinions to yourself sometimes," he said in a cold, steely voice. "I'm a grown-up—I can make my own decisions. I know you're upset that you couldn't help Jessica, but that doesn't mean you have to cram your advice down *my* throat!"

Elizabeth caught her breath sharply. She couldn't believe her ears. *Dana must have already warped Todd's mind for him to talk to me like that!*

"How *dare* you?" she seethed indignantly, clenching her fists in fury. "This has nothing to do with Jessica! Are you *that* blind, Todd? Don't you think it's a *little* suspicious that out of all the guys on this huge campus, Dana's going after *another* one of my exes?"

Todd's face registered shock, but Elizabeth was too incensed to stop the words from tumbling out. Diplomacy was a distant memory. "Dana doesn't care about you at all!" she went on. "She's just *using* you to get back at *me!*"

All the color had drained from Todd's face. He was staring in abject horror at some point behind her. Suddenly Elizabeth's skin crawled. She whirled and saw Dana Upshaw standing with her hands on her hips, staring at Elizabeth with blazing, murderous ire in her eyes.

For a second Dana thought she was having a nightmare. It was like a horror movie—just when she thought she was safe from Elizabeth Wakefield, the self-appointed paragon of virtue reared her blond-ponytailed head.

Is she trying *to ruin my life?* Dana wondered,

standing paralyzed with rage. *She's already suc-ceeded in making me a total outcast—why can't she just let it go? Why is she going out of her way to keep us from being happy?*

There was a long, tense silence. For a second Elizabeth stared at Dana wide-eyed, looking like a little girl with her hand caught in the cookie jar. Then she appeared to recover, and the slightest trace of a superior smirk touched her face, as if she was actually *glad* Dana had overheard her insults.

That was it. Dana saw red; the edges of her vision blurred.

"Listen, Elizabeth," she snapped, taking a step closer. "This isn't about you. It's about *me* and *Todd*. And we have *nothing* to prove to you. Get it?"

"I—I—," Elizabeth stammered, paling.

"Good," Dana spat. "Because you really need to work on getting your *own* life—and staying *out* of ours." She knew she should leave it at that, but all the months of bitter resentment toward Elizabeth were pouring out at once. Adrenaline was cours-ing through her.

"That way *we* can get on with our relationship," Dana went on, "and *you* can get on with being lonely and bitter . . . or whatever it is you do when you and Tom Watts aren't busy with your tedious little on-again, off-again love-hate drama."

Elizabeth's face contorted into several different shapes and even more shades of red before she threw up her hands. "Fine," she said disgustedly. "I won't stoop to your level by dignifying any of that with a response. I'll just leave you to your little *relationship*. And I certainly hope it *isn't* about me because I want nothing to do with it. As far as I'm concerned, you two deserve each other." With that, Elizabeth spun on her heel and stalked off.

All at once Dana was exhausted, overcome by the confrontation. Her legs felt like jelly. She glanced over at Todd for reassurance—and realized he was staring after Elizabeth, a stricken look on his face.

Todd still loves her, Dana thought in a panic. *He must hate me for blowing up at her like that!* Her heart lurched. Once again Elizabeth Wakefield had succeeded in destroying Dana's hopes for true love.

Jessica paced the upstairs hallway, trailing her fingertips languidly across the wallpaper. All along the wall, and up and down the staircase, hung pictures of the twins and their older brother, Steven.

She felt a wistful twinge as she stared into the small, heart-shaped faces of herself and her sister. The twins were so perfect and symmetrical as little girls in matching outfits. In a couple of the pictures Jessica almost couldn't tell who was who. Then as the twins grew, they split into separate entities: Jessica in purple and pink, her hair full of ribbons; Elizabeth ponytailed, in overalls.

I wish we could be the same like that again,

Jessica thought longingly. Vaguely she recalled that she'd been the one to insist matching outfits were dorky—but now they seemed like a beautiful way of showing how close the twins were. *Being a twin is so special,* Jessica thought dreamily as she drifted down the hall toward Elizabeth's bedroom.

Then grief stabbed at her. "We're supposed to be two halves of a whole, Liz," she whispered aloud into the open doorway. "So why aren't you here with me?"

No answer floated through the air. Drawn by some powerful instinctive force, Jessica stepped across the threshold into the charmed circle of Elizabeth's space. She opened the closet and ran her hands lovingly over all the familiar, faded fabrics that Elizabeth had worn in high school. Her sister's perfume even hung faintly over the clothes, mingled with must and mothballs. Jessica gathered a handful of shirtsleeves and burrowed her face into them, inhaling reverently.

"Why haven't you called, Liz? You feel so far away!" Anxiety nagged at her. Jessica rummaged through the closet, searching for something—anything—that would bring her closer to her twin.

Her eyes lit on a pale green polo shirt that Elizabeth used to wear almost every week in high school. A sudden urge struck her. Jessica tore off her pajama top and pulled Elizabeth's shirt over her head. She ran over to the dresser and pulled out pair after pair of frayed, vaguely dated-looking pants until she found the beige Dockers that Elizabeth had practically lived in when the twins were sixteen.

Jessica yanked down her pajama bottoms and stepped into the pants. They hung low on her hips—she hadn't had much of an appetite lately—but still fit all right. She grabbed a scrunchie off the dresser, pulled her hair back from her face, and twisted it into a ponytail. Then she bounded back to the closet and gazed into the full-length mirror that hung inside the door.

"Liz!" she exclaimed delightedly. "It's really you!"

Her sister's face beamed back at her.

"I love you," Jessica whispered, and the Elizabeth in the mirror mouthed the words along with her.

She reached out a tremulous hand to touch Elizabeth's face. But instead of her sister's soft skin, her fingertips encountered cold, smooth glass. Tears filled Jessica's eyes.

It's no use pretending, she realized despondently, her rib cage heaving with violent, soundless sobs. Her own twin didn't want to be her other half anymore. Why would Elizabeth abandon her like this?

Jessica crumpled into a heap on the floor and pressed her cheek against the cool, hard surface of the mirror. A horrible, sickening thought had occurred to her: *What if something's happened to her . . . like what happened to Nick?*

* * *

"Todd, I'm so sorry, I swear," Dana whispered, twisting her hands together anxiously. The tears were streaming down her face now—no doubt streaking her eyeliner, but Dana didn't care. Todd was still staring aghast at Elizabeth's rapidly receding back, now a speck in the distance. "Please, Todd, I didn't mean it."

He turned to her, an incredulous expression in his dark eyes. "Dana—"

"Oh, Todd, don't look at me like that; I can't stand it!" Dana cried. She felt as if her heart had shattered. This was it—it was all over. She'd destroyed the most magical relationship of her life. "Really, I didn't mean to sound so harsh. I know Elizabeth's your friend—I'll apologize if you want me to." She paused in midstream to take a quivering breath. "I just couldn't let her talk about us that way. Todd, I swear I would never—"

"Dana!" Todd cut her off. "Time out!"

She looked up, apprehensive, and did a double take. He was . . . grinning?

Todd placed his hands on her shoulders and gazed intently into her face, his coffee brown eyes warm. "Dana," he said softly, "I don't want you to apologize. I'm not mad at you. I was just shocked that Elizabeth would say those things to my face. I mean, she doesn't even know you! Who is she to say that what we have isn't real?"

"I just want you to hear me say this, Todd— I'm *not* using you to get back at Elizabeth, not at all," Dana insisted fervently. "That's the furthest thing from—"

"Shhh, Dana, I know." Gently Todd touched a silencing finger to her lips. The tender, trusting smile on his face was perhaps the sweetest sight Dana had ever seen. "Elizabeth is my friend, but any hold she had over me was a long time ago. I would never believe her over you—or over what my heart tells me about you. I'm honored that you would defend what we have."

Fresh tears welled up in Dana's eyes. For a moment she was so moved, she couldn't speak.

Todd folded her into his strong arms. Dana leaned her head against his broad shoulder, silently thanking her lucky stars that she had found the most understanding, accepting, loving guy in the world.

"I love you, Dana," Todd whispered huskily. "Unconditionally."

Dana tilted her tear-stained face to his. "I love you too, Todd."

He bent his head, and his lips found hers in a lingering kiss that started soft and gradually built in passion. At that moment Dana's heart was full to bursting. She felt closer to Todd than she'd ever felt to anyone in the world. And she had the feeling they'd be getting even closer very soon.

Chapter Eight

"Lonely and bitter, huh?" Elizabeth muttered angrily under her breath as she bent over an article on how to prepare for finals, which were just a few short weeks away. "Who does that little witch think she is?"

She bore down too hard on the newspaper galleys she was marking up, and the point of her pencil snapped off. Elizabeth glanced around, slightly embarrassed. The other student journalists in the *Sweet Valley Gazette* office were still working at their desks, off in their own deadline-driven worlds.

Elizabeth turned back to her work, willing herself to focus, but she couldn't stop stewing over Dana's words. *Lonely and bitter*—it fit neatly with Tom's "old maid" comments. *Am I really just a repressed, sexually frustrated goody two-shoes?*

"Well, at least I don't jump into bed with every guy who looks my way," she grumbled resentfully to herself. Even though her feelings for Todd had long since faded, there was something vexing about the thought of Dana sharing something Elizabeth had never known with *both* of the only *two* men Elizabeth had ever really loved.

"There you are, Wakefield. I've been looking all over for you."

Elizabeth glanced up, startled out of her glum thoughts by the voice of the *Gazette* editor in chief, Ed Greyson, who was hovering by her desk. "Oh, hi, Ed; sorry I'm late. I got a little sidetracked—"

"Never mind about that now. I've got a plum assignment for you." Ed was a hard-nosed journalist who always got right down to brass tacks— sometimes a little self-importantly, Elizabeth thought. "Have you heard of the cable network Intense?"

Elizabeth set aside her galleys. "Is that that new extreme-sports channel?"

Ed nodded. "Well, this summer they're sponsoring some kind of televised competition where teams of students go on a cross-country trip and compete in events to win prizes. The network is holding a two-day press conference in L.A. to drum up applicants, and I want you to cover it."

A puff piece on some TV station's publicity stunt? That's his plum assignment? Elizabeth thought, trying to keep the disappointment off her face. "Are you sure that story's right for me, Ed?" she asked politely. "Wouldn't that fall more into the sports department's territory?"

"The prizes are all generous scholarships," the editor explained. "This could be a great opportunity for some SVU students, and you're my top reporter for coverage of academic issues. I'm counting on you to get the word out." He rapped on Elizabeth's desk with his knuckles for emphasis. "Besides, it's a trip to L.A., all expenses paid. This is a great chance for you, Elizabeth."

Two days in L.A.? Elizabeth hesitated. She didn't want to let her boss down, but with Jessica's condition so precarious, and everything else in her life so chaotic, he couldn't have picked a worse time to send her out of town. "I don't know, Ed. I mean, I'm flattered that you thought of me, but really, with my classes and everything—"

"I didn't *think* of you; I'm *assigning* this to you." Ed's steely eyes were trained on Elizabeth. "We can work something out with your teachers for the classes you'll miss. But if you pass this one up, don't expect me to *think* of you the next time a big story like this comes along."

Elizabeth's shoulders sank in defeat. "OK, I'll do it," she agreed resignedly.

Well, I did promise myself I'd keep my distance from Jess, she reminded herself. If she was supposed to stay detached, what difference did it make if she was in Sweet Valley or in L.A.?

"Wyatt, over here! I'm open!" Tom crouched down low and cupped his hands wide. A few yards away Danny spotted him, nodded, and tossed the basketball his way. Tom caught it, dribbled, and went for the layup. The ball landed with a satisfying *swish* in the basket. Panting, Tom jogged away from the net and high-fived a couple of his nearby teammates.

"You're going down, Watts," promised Jim Washburn, a jovial Sigma, pointing a mock-warning finger at Tom as he dribbled the ball.

"In your dreams, Washburn," Danny crowed as he swooped past and stole the basketball. Tom watched in admiration as Danny, grinning broadly, sank a basket before anyone else had a chance to react. It was hard to believe that the alert, athletic guy scoring fast breaks was the same guy who had been strung out and stumbling around bars for the past week. Danny's skin had lost its greenish tinge and now shone a healthy, rich brown with perspiration.

Good call, Danno, Tom reflected as he sprinted across the court, guarding Evan Hart, another one of Danny's buddies. He wiped his brow with the already soaked hem of his T-shirt. It was as if he were sweating out some of his bitterness over Elizabeth.

"Think fast, Watts!" Danny called, hurling the ball at Tom. Tom caught it squarely and led the stampede back across the court. He faked left, ducked right to escape Jim Washburn's waving arms, and made another basket. Danny let out a victory cry as they slapped hands. He looked as if he was already on the road to recovery. Maybe he didn't need Tom's help. Maybe giving him Isabella's number would just set him back.

But if there was some way to get Elizabeth to speak to you and Danny knew about it, a little voice in Tom's head pointed out, *you'd never forgive* him *for not telling you.*

Evan scored a basket and then bent over with his hands on his knees, breathing hard. "Time out, guys. I'm getting too old for this."

Tom waved his hand to beckon Danny over. "Hey, man, can I talk to you a minute?"

Mrs. Wakefield looked up and gave a little start when Jessica padded into the doorway of her study. "Jess, what's wrong?" she exclaimed, getting up from her desk chair so quickly that it teetered backward. "Have you been crying?"

Jessica caught a glimpse of her reflection in the antique mirror on the study wall. She was still wearing Elizabeth's old clothes, now rumpled and disheveled. Her hair hung loose in ratty snarls around her face, and her eyes were swollen and red rimmed.

She turned slowly to her mother. "Mom, tell me the truth," she implored mournfully. "When is Liz coming home to visit me?"

"I . . . well . . ." Mrs. Wakefield's hand fluttered to her mouth, and her brows knotted in concern.

The walls of the study vibrated, radiating with the intensity of Jessica's need. Missing Elizabeth was like a jagged, gaping hole in her soul. Why couldn't her mother see that? "*Please,* Mom, I need to know," she begged. "Why hasn't she called? Why hasn't she come back? Doesn't she love me anymore?"

For a second Mrs. Wakefield's face was ashen. "Of *course* Elizabeth still loves you," she said quickly. Then her mouth stretched into a toothy smile that didn't reach her tired eyes. "Actually," she added brightly, "Elizabeth is coming home tomorrow! We're all having a special family dinner—Steven will be here too."

"Ohhh . . ." Jessica's knees went weak with relief. The corners of the room softened. She clutched the door frame for support. *Elizabeth just wanted to surprise me,* she realized, her terrors allayed. That's why she hadn't called back. Nothing bad had happened to her! Elizabeth still loved her!

"Now why don't you lie down and rest for a while, honey?" her mother said in a voice that made Jessica feel small and childlike. "You must be tired. Did you take your pill this afternoon?"

Jessica nodded dumbly. Now that she thought about it, she did feel sleepy. Exhausted, even. She could barely stand up on her own.

"Come on, let's get you into bed."

As her mother led her by the shoulder to her bedroom, Jessica could hardly keep her eyes open. It seemed as if she was *always* sleepy nowadays, ever since she'd started taking those pills.

But for once she didn't mind the thick, groggy cloud floating around her. Sleeping would make the time go by faster. And she couldn't wait to pass the hours until her twin arrived. Everything would be all right then.

"What's up, man?" Danny jogged across the basketball court and sat down beside Tom on the courtside wooden bench. He leaned back against the mesh fence and stretched out his aching legs, feeling as if his whole body were awash in an adrenaline-soaked glow.

Tom's shoulders were bent, and he was looking down at his hands. "Well, I kind of wanted to run something by you. See, I talked to Lila the other day. . . ."

Danny didn't particularly care about Lila. He was half listening, half basking in the afternoon sunlight. He couldn't remember the last time he'd been in such an upbeat mood.

"So she found the name of the hospital where Isabella—"

Danny shot upright, instantly attentive. "Huh? Isabella?" For the first time he noticed that Tom was holding a slip of paper in his hands. Danny narrowed his eyes and stared at his friend. "Run that by me again?"

Tom handed over the slip of paper. "There's her address and phone number in Switzerland. I hope you don't think I was overstepping my bounds, Danny. I just couldn't stand to see you so upset."

"Uh-huh." Danny was at a loss as to what else to say. He stared down at the slip of paper, holding it gingerly by the edges as if it were something delicate.

"But you know, it's up to you," Tom pointed out, sounding nervous. "You can crumple up that paper and throw it away right now if you want." He gave Danny a crooked grin. "Well, you probably shouldn't litter. But you know what I mean."

Danny cracked a smile. "Thanks, bro," he said, meeting Tom's eyes. "I'm not sure what to do about this, but don't worry—I know you were trying to do the right thing."

"That's a relief." Tom clapped Danny on the back. "I'll give you some time to think it over. Good luck, man."

As Tom jogged back onto the court, Danny remained slumped on the bench. Emotions churned inside him. He felt as if the piece of paper in his hands were a loaded gun. Just when he was starting to think he might be able to put Isabella behind him . . .

Deep down, Danny wasn't sure he could pass up this final chance to get in touch with the woman he loved. Calling might not bring Isabella back—but at least he could say good-bye. Maybe telling her he loved her one last time would give Danny the peace of mind to go on with his life once and for all.

"Let's see . . . pajamas, underwear, sneakers . . . ," Elizabeth murmured to herself as she lifted neat, folded piles off her bed and into her duffel bag. Should she bring a nice dress in case there was some kind of evening event?

"Might as well," she figured aloud, going over to her closet. She fingered a long, blue silk sheath that Jessica had frequently borrowed for dates with Nick. Unexpectedly a lump formed in her throat. Elizabeth let go of the dress and grabbed a maize-colored A-line off its hanger instead.

I guess I can't put off calling home any longer, she realized as she stuffed the dress into her bag. So far she had only mustered the nerve to return Jessica's calls once, and her father had told her Jessica was napping. But she couldn't leave for L.A. without checking in with her family. Elizabeth exhaled deeply before picking up the phone.

Mrs. Wakefield answered. "Liz! I was going to call you soon. Jessica was just asking for you."

"She was? Is she there?" Elizabeth felt her throat tighten nervously.

"Oh, she's lying down right now. I don't think it would be a good idea to disturb her."

Elizabeth let out her breath, then immediately felt guilty. "Well, tell her I send my love," she said lamely. "Listen, Mom, tomorrow I'm leaving for L.A. for a couple of days, but I promise I'll make it home soon."

"Tomorrow?" Her mother sounded chagrined. "Oh no, Liz! I told Jessica I was planning a special family dinner, and I promised her you'd be home. Steven already said he'd go out of his way to fit it in before a law exam. Can't you reschedule your trip?"

Hearing about how great her brother was only made Elizabeth feel like a worse sister. She ran a tense hand through her bangs. "I wish I could, Mom, but I have to cover a press conference for the *Gazette*. How come you didn't tell me about this dinner sooner?"

Her mother was silent for a second. "It just came up," she said at last. "Elizabeth, your sister really wants to see you. Isn't there anything you can do?"

Blades of guilt were twisting in Elizabeth's gut. "Well, what if I come home for the weekend?" she suggested. "As soon as I get back from L.A., I'll head straight home. And you can call me at the conference if you need me."

112

"All right, Elizabeth; that sounds good," her mother said in a weary voice. "I know Jessica will be glad to have you for the whole weekend. I'll figure out something to tell her about tomorrow."

Is she trying *to guilt-trip me?* Elizabeth wondered. She felt bad enough already.

She gave her mother the name and number of the hotel in L.A. "You'd better just call the front desk and have the hotel staff page me if I'm not in my room," Elizabeth added with a glance at her itinerary. "It looks like I'm going to be running around to a million different events."

"OK, Elizabeth. I'm going to get dinner started, but I'll talk to you soon. We love you, dear."

"Love you too." Elizabeth hung up, feeling a million miles away from her family. Jessica needed her, and she wasn't there.

It's not like my life is just going to stop because Jessica's not well, Elizabeth rationalized. But no matter how she reasoned with herself, she couldn't shake the terrible feeling, deep in her bones, that she was letting her family down.

"Make yourself at home. Can I get you anything?" Todd asked as he closed the door of his dorm room.

"No, I'm fine." Dana stood in the center of the small, carpeted room, the pit of her stomach doing back flips. After the way she and Todd had bonded today, Dana had been sure the time was right. But now that they were really here together, a million questions were circling in her mind.

What if it's too soon?

What if it changes things between us?

What if he's disappointed?

What if I'm *disappointed?*

Todd was over by the stereo, his back turned. Dana did a quick scan of what she was wearing—a purple silk shirt loosely knotted over black leggings. *Looks OK,* she decided. *My hair's in place and everything. I'm wearing clean underwear.* And the box of condoms was tucked in the purse she'd slung on a chair. All systems were go. So why was she shaking like a leaf?

Todd turned back to her with a sly grin as music started to play—a scratchy old jazz record. "Billie Holiday," he explained, coming toward Dana. "Shall we dance?"

"Right here?" Dana laughed as Todd swept her into his arms. One of his hands pressed gently against the small of her back, sending delicious shivers up her spine. The other hand cupped hers delicately as he led her in slow circles around the room. Dana giggled and crooked her free arm around Todd's neck.

"OK, I'm going to attempt a difficult maneuver," Todd said gravely. "Please make sure your seat belt is completely fastened." He let go of Dana's waist and spun her out along his arm.

Dana whirled back in, her back fitting snugly

against Todd's chest, and tilted her chin up to smile at him. "Not bad, Wilkins. Not bad at all."

He took her in his arms again, and this time as they moved together across the room, he gave her a soft, searching kiss. Then his lips trailed away, tracing a chain of little kisses down her neck. Dana felt her breath start to come faster, desire building up inside her. She could tell how slow, how careful he was being; he could probably sense how nervous she was. *He really wants this to be special,* she realized. And somehow, just knowing that, Dana didn't feel quite so nervous anymore.

When Todd's mouth reached the hollow of her throat, he slipped her blouse off her shoulders and continued trailing kisses all the way down her arm. He let go of her fingertips, and Dana reached out to unbutton Todd's collared shirt. They stepped apart long enough to let their shirts fall to the floor.

Standing there in her black satin bra, Dana felt momentarily self-conscious. Then in another instant they were kissing urgently, furiously. The feel of Todd's bare skin against hers and his scent—soapy clean with a hint of musk—was exhilarating. Dana ran her palms down his muscle-rippled back, no longer sure whether they were still spinning in a slow dance—or if she was just dizzy with passion. Their bodies fit together perfectly; every one of Dana's pores tingled with delight.

"OK, one more ambitious move." Todd took

Dana's hand in his again and wrapped her waist in the curve of his arm. He leaned over to dip her, and Dana tilted back . . . too far. She lost her balance, and together they tumbled in a heap on the bed, collapsing in laughter.

"I've never been very good at dipping," Todd admitted apologetically.

"I think you did just fine," Dana whispered with a shy smile as she gazed into his warm eyes. As Todd's lips lingered on hers, she felt utterly at ease; all her anxiety had washed away.

Dana's heart told her that this was sublimely right—what she and Todd had was precious. She trusted him completely. And she knew she would remember this night for the rest of her life.

Chapter Nine

"Forget everything you know about extreme sports," demanded a preternaturally perky redhead as she banged her fists on the podium for emphasis. She jabbed her finger at the rows of assembled reporters. "The Intense network's college competition is wild. It's edgy. It's *in your face!*"

I wish you would get out *of my face,* Elizabeth told the redhead silently, stifling a yawn as she turned over a sheet in her notepad. She'd been listening to superbuff, hyper-enthusiastic people gush about their stupid competition for over two hours. And so far this press conference had taught her nothing she couldn't have learned from a two-page press release—except that it was actually possible for humans to spew meaningless catchphrases for ten minutes straight without pausing for breath.

"We have lined up the craziest, most hard-core

events the world has ever seen," the redhead was saying, practically bouncing up and down behind the microphone stand. "And we're looking for some sporty, spontaneous, *sexy* students to take a trip with us—and win unbelievable prizes!"

Maybe she's not human, Elizabeth mused. *If she is, I don't even want to* know *what kind of drugs she's on.*

A dull explosion of static burst from the loudspeaker overhead. "Paging Elizabeth Wakefield," a voice crackled. "Elizabeth Wakefield, please report to the front desk."

A few people turned to stare at Elizabeth as she bolted out of her seat and scurried out of the conference room, but she didn't care. *Something's happened to Jessica!* was all she could think.

But as soon as Elizabeth rounded the corner of the hotel corridor and headed to the front desk, she instantly realized it wasn't her family who had paged her after all.

"Mike!" Elizabeth gasped. He was standing by the hotel desk, looking shockingly handsome in his leather bomber jacket and jeans. "What are you doing here?"

"I'm sorry I didn't call first, Elizabeth," Mike said, pushing a lock of hair out of his eyes. "No, make that I'm sorry I haven't called in a while. I was tied up with some family stuff, but I just had to see you. I called your number at the newspaper, and they told me you were here working. So if you want me to go, just say the word."

"No, no—you're not interrupting anything, really," Elizabeth said hastily. She couldn't help breaking out into a grin. In spite of her confusion about Mike, it was a relief to know he didn't completely hate her. And his gorgeous, tanned face certainly was a sight for sore eyes after two hours of mindless conference filler. Her relationship with Mike might be a lot of things, but it certainly wasn't boring.

Mike returned her smile and reached out to squeeze her shoulders. "Well, if you're not busy, I was hoping we could spend some time together tonight. Maybe I can show you the town."

A night alone in L.A. with Mike? Elizabeth hesitated, her heart pounding. *Anything could happen.* Maybe it wasn't such a good idea. Still, it was awfully cute of him to come all the way out to see her. Why not make the most of the trip?

"That sounds great," she said. "The press events end around six."

"I'll pick you up around seven, then." Mike leaned in to give her a peck on the cheek. Impulsively Elizabeth planted a quick kiss on his lips. Mike looked pleasantly surprised.

Elizabeth's heart was doing somersaults as she turned to head back to the conference room. She had no idea where she and Mike were headed. But in L.A., with campus and Calico Drive and everything else seeming far away, unpredictable didn't seem like such a bad thing. *After all,* she reasoned as she hurried down the hall, *wasn't a spontaneous fling exactly what I wanted to take my mind off my problems?*

The doorbell roused Jessica from the sound, dark sleep of her afternoon nap. She opened her eyes, absorbing the dim grayness and the sensation that hours had passed without her. Downstairs she could hear voices—her father's deep, hearty one and her mother's lighter one, lifted in excitement.

"Elizabeth's here!" Jessica whispered aloud. She scrambled out of bed and barreled downstairs, still in her pajamas. "Liz, I'm so hap—"

Jessica stopped in her tracks at the bottom of the stairs. Her brother, Steven, was sitting next to her father on the couch; they looked strangely like clones with their dark brown hair and white collared shirts. Mrs. Wakefield was standing a few feet away, looking nervously at Jessica.

"Hey, Jess!" Steven got up and ran to wrap her in a big bear hug. "It's great to see you. How's my little sister?"

"I'm OK," Jessica said, feebly returning his hug. Her muscles felt weak, limp from sleep. All the energy had drained out of her as soon as she realized Elizabeth wasn't at the door. "Thanks for coming to see me."

"Are you kidding?" Steven rumpled her hair. "I came for the free dinner! I heard Mom pulled out all the stops."

"It certainly smells delicious," Mr. Wakefield put in. "I'm starved—is it time for dinner yet, Alice?"

"Everything's just about ready," Mrs. Wakefield chirped.

Still dazed from her nap, Jessica felt as if she had stepped into a parallel universe, where her family had become characters on some black-and-white TV show. Everyone seemed as if they were trying so hard to be happy. But something wasn't right. Someone was missing.

"Wait," Jessica said slowly. "We can't eat until Elizabeth gets here."

Nobody said anything. Trepidation settled in Jessica's stomach. Then Mrs. Wakefield clapped. "Let's all go in the dining room!" she urged. "I want to show you something, Jessica."

Her mother found Jessica's hand and led her into the dining room, Mr. Wakefield and Steven filing behind. Jessica saw that the table was set with the good linen tablecloth and glowing candles. Orange blossoms overflowed from a crystal vase in the center of the table.

"See, isn't this fun?" Mrs. Wakefield exclaimed. "It's like we're all having a fancy night out without leaving the house!"

The candles cast strange, flickering shadows on the ceiling. The four gleaming, white china plates

121

laid out on the table looked to Jessica like gaping, open mouths. She could almost hear them screaming, *Where's Elizabeth?*

"And guess what?" her mother was saying. "We have all your favorites! I made honey-mustard chicken, garlic mashed potatoes, grilled asparagus. . . ."

But Jessica wasn't listening. She was staring at the plates. One, two, three, four. Mom, Dad, Jessica . . . Steven. No place for Elizabeth.

Jessica looked up and stared squarely at her parents. "She's not coming, is she?"

Her mother's face fell. Her father's expression was dark.

Steven winced. "Jess, Liz had to go out of town at the last minute. Something came up at the *Gazette*."

"She *what?*" Jessica screeched. Out of town? Elizabeth wouldn't do that to her! They had to be lying. It was like a cruel joke.

Mrs. Wakefield rushed over to put an arm around Jessica. "It's going to be all right, dear. Elizabeth is going to come for the whole weekend. Won't that be great?"

"Great?" Jessica cried bitterly, tugging at fistfuls of her hair in frustration. "How can you say that?" The weekend was a million years away. Elizabeth was supposed to be there *tonight*—and she *always* kept her promises! It didn't make sense. Something was terribly wrong.

She grasped her mother's sleeve and tugged

hard, twisting the fabric in her hands with all the strength she had left. "Tell me the truth," she begged. *"Where's my sister?"*

Alice Wakefield's face registered shock, almost fear. Ned Wakefield moved between them, prying Jessica's white-knuckled fingers from her mother's arm. "Elizabeth is out of town, Jess," he repeated. "She's *fine!*"

The faces of her mother, her father, her brother swirled around Jessica in a blur. *All lying . . . all hiding something . . .* Jessica's chest was heaving up and down like a coiled spring, but no air was reaching her lungs. How could they stand there and tell her to her face that Elizabeth would just disappear like that?

"Something awful must have happened to her," she said with a moan, sinking to the floor. Her eyes were fluttering shut. Everything was melting into gray. "Something awful, just like . . ."

Jessica trailed off, unable to voice the sickening conclusion aloud: . . . *just like what happened to Nick.*

"So, was I right, Liz?" Mike asked as he stretched an arm across the backseat of his Corvette. His eyes twinkled in the moonlight. "Was it everything you anticipated and more?"

"The best milk shake I ever tasted," Elizabeth agreed solemnly. "And those cheese fries were highly addictive. It's a good thing I don't live in L.A., or my diet would be shot."

123

"Diet?" Mike snorted. "Women never cease to amaze me. You don't need to diet, Liz." His eyes softened, and he gave Elizabeth a lingering look that made her cheeks warm. "You're stunning just the way you are," he added in a lower voice, letting his outstretched arm slip onto her shoulders.

Elizabeth smiled, feeling her blush spread into a warm glow of happiness. Mike was being so sweet tonight. There was something awfully endearing about the fact that he'd suggested the 1950s-style drive-in diner, with its pink-and-blue neon lights bathing the parking lot in an enchanting radiance. It was nice to be with a guy who would take her someplace fun and quaint and totally unpretentious. *Tom would probably think a place like this was cheesy,* she couldn't help thinking. Then again, Tom would never be able to pull off driving a Corvette convertible either.

The poodle-skirted waitress roller-skated over to the car. "Can I get you anything else?"

"Just the check would be fine," Mike said. "I think we have a few more sights to see tonight." His eyes met Elizabeth's. "I want to take you on a drive down the coast, if that's cool. The view is totally incredible."

"Sure, that sounds like fun." Elizabeth squeezed his knee affectionately, a little surprised at how easy and natural the casual, intimate gesture felt. Maybe it was the nostalgia-themed restaurant that made her feel as if she'd stepped outside of time, or maybe it was just the thrill of being in a different city that made her problems seem far away and small. Whatever the cause, she was definitely relaxing around Mike. It seemed ridiculous that just yesterday she'd been more or less assuming she would never see him again.

Her eyes traveled from the chiseled line of Mike's jaw to the chest muscles that strained the fabric of his white, V-neck T-shirt. "You know, the view from right here is pretty spectacular too," she added boldly, lowering her lashes.

Mike raised his eyebrows in a mock-incredulous look. "Why, Miss Wakefield! Are you . . . coming on to me?"

Elizabeth giggled. "I think the milk shake must have gone to my head."

Her heart gave a little flutter as Mike leaned in to kiss her. As his strong arms wrapped around her, she felt safe, protected from all the stress and guilt that had been eating away at her back in Sweet Valley.

Mike may be a little rough around the edges, she thought dreamily as they kissed. *But he really has a good heart.* So maybe he wasn't the great love of her life—that didn't mean they had no future together, did it?

Not every guy has to be the be-all and end-all of my life, Elizabeth resolved, shivering deliciously as Mike's fingertips glided across the back of her neck. *So what if what we have is mostly physical? It*

125

just proves I'm not *the uptight prude* some *people think I am!*

With Mike nibbling at her ear, his breath warm on her skin, the decision was easy. For once in her life, she was just going to do what felt good.

"So I did OK on the midterm," Steven said over the clatter of silverware. "But I think the final is really going to be a killer. The professor has a reputation for throwing out questions on stuff we barely covered in class."

Jessica stifled a yawn and glanced up from the food she was pushing around on her plate to see if anyone had noticed. Her parents were nodding at Steven, chewing and swallowing without lowering the polite half smiles plastered on their faces. Jessica could sense the silent tension crackling under Steven's steady stream of chatter about his course work. Her family seemed so fragile and false, like a mirror reflecting nothing but blank space. Jessica half believed that if their frozen smiles fell, their faces might crack and shatter.

"I'm sure you'll do just fine, Steven," Mrs. Wakefield said encouragingly. Jessica lowered her head again. With her fork she shaped her uneaten mound of mashed potatoes into the form of an angel.

"Well, you never know," Steven was saying in a conversational tone Jessica had heard him use with acquaintances at parties. "Sometimes just figuring out what to study is half the battle—you have to kind of guess what the prof's thinking."

Carefully Jessica patted the two sides into broad wings. *Does my angel have wings?* she mused. She couldn't recall what they looked like. . . . *But he must—how else could he have reached my window?*

"It's funny," Steven continued, "just the other week I was talking about this class with Elizabeth, and she said—"

Mr. Wakefield cleared his throat loudly, and Steven paused in midstream. "Oh, I mean—what I meant to say was . . . ," he stammered. "I mean, I was talking to my *friend,* and . . ." Steven lapsed lamely into silence.

Jessica sensed that she was being watched, and not by a guardian spirit. Slowly she raised her face to meet her family's gaze. They were sitting frozen in place, staring at her with something like dread. There was no sound in the room, no movement of forks or knives—it was as if her parents and brother were all holding their breath at the same time.

They think I'm going to freak out, Jessica realized. Her hand shook as she set down her fork. *They think just hearing Elizabeth's name is going to drive me insane!*

Part of her wanted to reassure her family, to tell them that she wasn't crazy. But no words could move past the lump in her throat. It hurt inexpressibly to see her family staring at her as if she were a stranger—as if she were *sick*.

Jessica let out a choked sob and pushed back her chair. She ran to her room, blinded by tears, her flailing arms trailing along the walls to guide her. Throwing herself on her bed, Jessica burst into convulsive tears.

"Don't you see, Elizabeth?" she sobbed aloud to the empty room. "Don't you understand why I need you so badly?" Elizabeth wouldn't treat her like a child or like some kind of invalid. Elizabeth wouldn't walk on eggshells around her—she would talk to Jessica like a human being. She would listen—she would understand.

"I *know* you would understand." Jessica moaned into her pillow. "Where *are* you, Liz? You're the only one who can help me!"

The warm night breeze ruffled Mike's hair as the Corvette sped, top down, along the freeway. Leaning her elbow on her headrest, Elizabeth propped her cheek on her hand and sat admiring his achingly handsome profile. The coastline view of the hills, the waves crashing on the shore, and the glittering canopy of stars above had been as beautiful as Mike had promised . . . but Elizabeth could hardly tear her eyes off him.

"Here we are," Mike said, yanking the emergency brake. The engine shuddered to a halt, and Elizabeth realized with a little start that they had pulled up in front of the hotel.

Mike's gold-flecked eyes searched her face. "So, I guess this is good-bye." There was a question in his voice.

Elizabeth hesitated. She was having such a good time with Mike, she didn't want the night to end. But if she invited him up to her room, they would be alone together—anything could happen. And besides, she really did have to get up early for the conference. . . .

Frigid old maid, Tom's voice jeered in her mind.

Elizabeth let a smile uncurl slowly on her face. "Would you like to come up for a while?" she asked silkily.

Mike's face was a study in nonchalance. "Sure, I'd love to."

When they reached the door to her room, Elizabeth had trouble keeping her hands steady enough to put the passkey through the electronic lock. Inside her rib cage was a flurry of nervous anticipation.

As soon as the door closed behind them, Mike enfolded her in his arms, crushing her chest against his. Elizabeth tangled her fingers in his hair as they kissed. Mike's hands circled her back, caressed her shoulders, ran down her sides, burning a trail of fire everywhere they touched. Elizabeth felt dizzy, light-headed; she might not have been capable of standing on her own if Mike's touch hadn't kept her body firmly locked with his.

Her lips were stung raw and tingling when Mike drew back, his breath ragged. Elizabeth was about to move toward him again when he cleared his throat.

"Liz, not to kill the mood," Mike said in a low, soft tone, "but I kind of forgot to bring protection. Do you have any?"

Elizabeth felt as if she had suddenly been transported from a tropical island into a meat freezer. "Pro-Protection?" she sputtered, disentangling from Mike's embrace.

Mike looked taken aback. "Yeah, sorry—I know it's lame not to be prepared," he said in his normal voice, the romantic spell evaporating fast. "But it's not a big deal, right? I mean, the hotel must have a store or something."

"N-No big deal at all," Elizabeth squeaked, her voice an octave higher than usual. Her head was spinning. What was she doing?

Well, what did you expect *to happen when you invited Mike up?* a little voice in her head reproached. *Reality check! Guy plus girl plus hotel room—do the math!*

All the same, it hadn't really hit her until this moment that she had to make one of the most important decisions of her life—right now.

"I'll run down to the lobby," Elizabeth offered, stalling for time. "I think I did see a store there. Be right back."

She slipped out of the room quickly before Mike had a chance to respond. She needed some air—some time to clear her head. Mike was an amazing guy. Mike was an amazingly *sexy* guy. But she'd always imagined her first time would be with someone she truly loved.

Elizabeth broke into a run down the hotel hallway, as if she could flee from her conflicted emotions. Was she really ready to take that step? Or more realistically—was she that desperate?

"Jessica?" A soft knock sounded against the door frame. "Can I come in?"

Lying on her stomach on the bed, Jessica lifted her tear-stained face from where it was buried in Prince Albert's fur. Mrs. Wakefield was standing in the doorway, a nervous expression crimping her face.

She's afraid of me, Jessica thought. Exhausted from her evening pill, she stared dully at her mother, bereft of any words to express how isolated and sad she felt.

After a long pause Mrs. Wakefield took a tentative step forward. "I'm sorry to disturb you, honey. But your father and I were talking, and we thought you should have this."

Weakly, Jessica reached out a weary arm to accept the slip of paper her mother offered. *Elizabeth* was written on it, along with a phone number and the words *Los Angeles Hilton, room 203*.

Mrs. Wakefield was standing by Jessica's bed, wringing her hands. "You can ask her yourself about this weekend." Her voice quavered a little. "And Jess,

I'm so sorry for getting your hopes up about tonight."

Jessica's lips parted to form the words, *It's OK, Mom,* but somehow she couldn't find the energy to make the sound. Mrs. Wakefield turned, wiping away a tear as she left the room.

In an instant all Jessica's energy returned. Hurriedly she jumped up to shut the door after her mother, then she grabbed the cordless phone off the nightstand. Her fingers trembled as she dialed the number. It rang once, twice, three times as Jessica paced fitfully across her room. Prince Albert followed her attentively with his eyes, thumping his tail on the bed.

"Los Angeles Hilton, how may I help you?" a crisp, efficient female voice chirped at last.

"Can I talk to Elizabeth Wakefield?" Jessica asked breathlessly. "Room 203."

"Hold, please." There was an abrupt click, followed by a swell of synthesized classical music. Jessica licked her parched lips and made another circle around her room, fighting the groggy cloud that threatened to swallow her up. She had to be alert for this. Finally, after all this time, she was about to hear her sister's soothing voice. Finally Elizabeth would make everything all right.

The receptionist came back on the line. "I'm sorry, miss, but the gentleman of the room has requested that we hold all calls. May I take a message?"

"Gentleman?" Jessica choked. "What gentleman?" Nightmare images loomed in her mind—

shadowy, menacing men doing unimaginably terrible things to Elizabeth. *Just like what they did to Nick!* She squeezed her eyes shut, trying to blot out the awful pictures.

"I'm afraid I can't answer that for you, ma'am," the receptionist responded, sounding ominously, soullessly chipper. *Does she know something?* Jessica wondered wildly.

"Please, you have to let me talk to my sister," she begged. Blood was roaring in her ears, her pulse crashing like waves. "It's an emergency!"

The receptionist's voice had taken on an impatient tone. "I'm sorry; we were told to hold all calls. But I'd be happy to take a message."

"No!" Jessica realized she was shouting now, but she couldn't stop herself. She gripped the phone as if she were wringing the receptionist's neck. "No, no, no! I need to talk to her *now!*"

The response was a cruelly sharp click, then a jeering dial tone. Stunned, Jessica let the phone slip from her hand and crash to the floor.

Candy bars, sunscreen, shoe shine, mending kits . . . condoms. Elizabeth stopped in front of the display and glanced nervously around. All the other customers in the hotel pharmacy seemed to be going about their business, but Elizabeth felt as if a neon sign over her head were announcing why she was there.

Why am *I here?* she asked herself. *Is this really*

133

what I want? She wasn't even sure she wanted Mike as a boyfriend, much less as her first lover. An unwanted thought made her shudder—it wasn't so long ago that Mike had been *Jessica's* first lover.

Elizabeth took off down the aisle again, propelled by a gnawing sense of shame. *Mike and Jessica were really in love,* she realized, cringing. *They were* married, *for crying out loud! What kind of person would betray her own twin that way?* And to think she'd felt justified in condemning Todd and Dana's relationship—*that* was certainly less inappropriate than moving in on her twin's ex-husband! Especially with Jessica in the shape she was in . . . If she found out, it would kill her.

She stopped in front of the condom display again, her heart heavy with the sinking realization that she had to break things off with Mike. Having a physical relationship just for fun was one thing, but she'd chosen the most wrong person possible. *And all because of what Tom said to me,* she berated herself. Who cared what he thought anyway? Showing up an obnoxious ex-boyfriend was *not* the right reason to have sex for the first time.

"Can I help you find something, miss?"

Elizabeth whirled to see a pimply, teenage clerk standing behind her. "Uh, no, I—no," she stammered, her face flaming hot. "Excuse me."

She rushed past him and out of the store, embarrassment, guilt, and dread churning in her stomach. Now all she had to do was find her way out of this mess before somebody got hurt.

Sleep blurred the gray edges of Jessica's vision, although she couldn't remember when she had sunk onto her bed. But every time she let her eyes flicker shut, torturous visions assaulted her: Elizabeth screaming; Elizabeth lying cold and motionless, just like Nick; and—almost worst of all— Elizabeth smiling, laughing, not caring a bit that she had abandoned Jessica.

Jessica wrenched open her eyes. Her room seemed smaller than she remembered. Was it shrinking, closing in on her? She couldn't tell— her head was filled with fog. Dimly she could still hear the siren sound of the phone receiver on the floor. *If you would like to make a call, please hang up and try again. . . .*

Suddenly she desperately needed to get out, to breathe fresh air. Unsteadily she rose, staggered toward the door. Prince Albert scampered faithfully at her heels.

Somehow her feeble legs buoyed her downstairs and all the way out to the back porch. Then her knees gave way, and Jessica collapsed onto the wooden planks of the deck. She leaned back against a banister, and Prince Albert laid his head in her lap.

In spite of everything, Jessica smiled. "You still love me, don't you, Albert?" Her hands threaded the thick fur of the dog's neck. "You're the only one who doesn't think I'm crazy." A fat tear rolled down her face and burst on her jawline. "Even Elizabeth gave up on me. She doesn't even care anymore—that's why she won't come to see me."

Prince Albert looked up at her with sad, understanding eyes. Jessica's whole body was racked with a heaving sob. "What am I going to do? My own twin's abandoned me." The tears were coming fast and furious now, stinging her face in the cool night breeze. "Without Liz, I have nothing. *Nothing!* What point is there in going on anymore?" Jessica hung her head, weeping uncontrollably as waves of pain buffeted her weary frame.

Then suddenly she felt Prince Albert's back arch under her hands. A second later the dog had slipped from her grasp. Jessica looked up to see him facing out toward the darkened yard, his tail flattened warily. He gave a sharp, warning bark.

"What is it, boy?" Shakily Jessica drew herself up to stand and wiped the tears from her face with her pajama top. She stepped off the porch and squinted out into the shadows. What she saw made her heart leap in her chest.

A few yards away, half concealed behind a tree, loomed a tall figure, his features imperceptible in the darkness.

"It's *you!*" Jessica breathed ecstatically, taking a step toward her angel.

Chapter
Ten

"What took you so long?" Mike murmured, wrapping his strong arms around Elizabeth almost before she could shut the hotel room door. "I was starting to think you'd forgotten about me."

Elizabeth felt her body melting into his embrace, her lips aching for his searing kiss. But Jessica's face, hurt and pleading, hovered before her eyes. Straightening her spine, Elizabeth pushed Mike firmly away. "We need to talk."

Mike looked surprisingly unsurprised, "Every guy's four least favorite words in the English language." He sat down on the bed. "OK, shoot."

Elizabeth took a deep, shaky breath. "Listen, Mike, I really like you. . . ." She twisted her hands together helplessly.

"But?" Mike prompted.

"But I've been doing some thinking, and it really isn't right to do this to Jessica." Elizabeth

saw him wince at her sister's name. "Deep down, I think we both know that. Spending time with you is a lot of fun, but it's not worth hurting her. Nothing is."

Mike nodded seriously. Elizabeth was startled to realize that he actually looked relieved.

"You're absolutely right, Liz. And the stupid thing is, I was thinking the exact same thing." Mike heaved a sigh and ran a hand through his tousled hair. "After the night when you showed up at my door, I started feeling really weird about being with you. That's why I didn't call for a while—I just needed to sort things out in my head. And finally I decided we were together for all the wrong reasons."

"So why did you come to see me here?" Elizabeth asked.

"Actually, I came to tell you it was over—I just felt like I had to set things straight right away. But then you seemed so glad to see me. . . ." Mike grinned sheepishly. "I'm sure this isn't a news flash, but guys are weak. I've been kind of lonely since Jess and I split up, and I guess I figured, as long as you were into it . . ." He shrugged, and Elizabeth felt her face flush. "Well, anyway, I honestly am glad you spoke up before things went too far."

"I'm sorry about all this," Elizabeth said uncomfortably. "I should have figured out sooner it wasn't going to work."

"I'm sorry too." Mike stood up and grabbed

his jacket off a chair. He walked over to the door and put his hands on Elizabeth's shoulders. "Listen, Liz, I know we weren't meant to be together, but I really do care about you . . . and your sister. If you ever need anything—either of you—just call, OK? I'll come running."

"Thanks," Elizabeth said, not quite able to meet Mike's eyes. She knew he was sincere, and she was grateful that he was being so understanding. But his touch still felt strange, still stirred feelings she no longer wanted to feel.

"Don't worry; I'm leaving." Mike gave her a quick peck on the cheek. She held open the door for him, and he paused in the doorway and turned. "Take care of yourself, Liz. And take care of Jessica too."

"OK, I will," Elizabeth said awkwardly. "Bye."

She closed the door and leaned back against it, sagging with an overwhelming mix of relief and alarm. Sure, she'd stopped things before they went too far, but it was unnerving to know just how close she'd come to . . .

Elizabeth buried her face in her hands and shook her head, as if to purge the utterly inappropriate urges that had possessed her. *What's wrong with me?* she wondered, distraught. How could she even have *considered* losing her virginity to her sister's ex-husband? The whole situation was such a mess—it was as if her life was spinning out of control.

I can't let anything like this happen again, Elizabeth told herself sternly. No more being selfish. No more atrocious judgment calls. Starting now, she had to pull myself together. For the sake of her sanity . . . and Jessica's.

"Come closer!" Jessica cried as she staggered across the lawn, her arms outstretched. "Please, just let me see your face!"

The spirit had taken a few steps toward her, but his face was still a dark gray blank. She forced her bone-weary legs to keep moving. "Please, I just want to look at you!"

"Jessica!" her brother's voice barked behind her. Jessica whirled to see Steven standing on the porch. His face registered anger, and he took off across the yard.

She turned back toward the angel, but it was too late—he was speeding away, receding into the darkness and the distance. *"Nooo!"* she cried, her hands still reaching out to grasp empty air. "Don't go! Don't leave me!"

Steven passed by her in a rush, and Jessica frantically grabbed ahold of his shirttail. "Don't, Steven—he's my guardian angel," she sobbed. "He watches out for me!"

Steven stared at her, aghast. "Jess, that was just some creep spying on you!" He glanced in the direction the angel had gone; Jessica followed his gaze and saw only darkness.

Steven swore under his breath. "I'll never catch him now. Come on, Jess, let's get you inside and call 911."

"B-But he wasn't going to hurt me!" Jessica insisted as her brother led her by the arm back to the house.

"You don't know that, Jess," Steven said through gritted teeth. "Believe me, guys who hide in backyards are no angels."

Inside, the light was too bright. Everything had too-sharp edges. Her mother and father swarmed around Jessica, their faces white as ghosts, clamoring too fast for her to comprehend. Jessica was crying as Mrs. Wakefield lowered her into a chair at the kitchen table.

Steven was already on the phone. "Hello, I'd like to report a prowler. . . ."

"But it *wasn't* a prowler!" Jessica sobbed, her face in her hands. "It was an angel—the angel who watches over me." It was too much to bear—they had driven away her spirit guardian, her only ray of hope. What if he was angry at her now? What if he never came back?

"Shhh, honey, it's going to be all right." Her mother's voice. Jessica felt hands rubbing slow circles on her back. "That wasn't an angel; it was just a man."

"It must have been a real person—Steven saw him too, remember?" her father's voice put in. "Maybe you just imagined you saw an angel."

"Maybe you dreamed it," her mother suggested. The circles on Jessica's back turned to pats. "Remember, like the other night, when you had a bad dream?"

"But he's real! I've seen him before . . . ," Jessica whispered through her fingers, then trailed off. Suddenly she was confused. She'd been asleep the night she saw the angel with Nick's face . . . but she'd woken up when he called her name. Hadn't she?

Maybe I did *dream it,* she thought, lifting her bewildered face. *But I couldn't have dreamed* all *the times I saw him . . . could I?*

She rifled through the cluttered drawers of her memory, but she couldn't seem to recall a daytime vision of the angel. It was so hard, when her head was a fog . . . when she was so sleepy all the time. *Ever since I started taking those pills,* she thought in frustration. *Everything is so fuzzy.* She just couldn't be sure what was real anymore.

"Do you think if we ordered a pizza, we would have to put on our clothes?" Dana asked innocently.

Todd chuckled as he ran his finger along the side of Dana's face. Lying against his pillows with her disarrayed mahogany curls framing her face, wearing nothing but the sheets, she looked radiantly beautiful. "Well, if *you* go to the door, I'm

142

sure the pizza guy wouldn't mind. I bet we wouldn't even have to tip him."

Dana sighed and thumped her feet impatiently under the covers. "I don't want to get out of bed," she said in a pouty-little-girl voice, "but I'm starving all of a sudden!"

Todd propped himself onto his elbows. He smoothed a tendril of hair off Dana's forehead and kissed the spot where the curl had been. "Well, we haven't eaten since . . . what time did we order that Chinese food? Midnight?"

Dana gave him a sly smile, her eyes twinkling. "Where does the time go?"

Todd was grinning as he lowered his face to kiss her. Dusky light filtered through the blinds, shrouding the dorm room in a smoky glow. They had been tangled in Todd's bed for almost a whole day now. Between spells of drifting off to sleep, they'd been alternately talking for hours . . . and getting to know each other in other ways.

"You know, I could really get used to this lifestyle," Todd said, tracing the contours of Dana's moistened lips with his fingertip. "All Dana, all the time. No homework, no classes—and no clothes."

Dana giggled and stretched her arms languorously over her head. "I'm with you. I guess we better start playing the lottery now, huh? We won't need an education when we're off on our yacht, traveling the world." She hooked her arms around Todd's neck, her eyes sparkling playfully.

"Where should we buy our mansion, *dahling?*"

"I don't care, as long as it's far away from this campus." Todd scratched his chin, pretending to contemplate the question seriously. "Maybe we'll have a château in Paris, a bungalow on the South Seas. . . ."

"Mmmm, and a villa in Venice." Dana's smile faded suddenly, her hazel eyes full of wistful longing. "Can you imagine, Todd? I mean, not all that fantasy-lifestyle stuff, but just starting over somewhere new—someplace we could truly make our own. Leaving behind all the bad memories— wouldn't that be heavenly?"

"Making a fresh start with the most beautiful, funny, talented woman in the world? Yeah, I'd say that would pretty much be paradise." Todd felt his stomach rumble. "But right now I'd settle for a pepperoni pizza."

Dana's eyes were shining with affection as she pulled his face close to hers. "Pizza can wait," she said throatily.

At three o'clock in the morning the corridors of Dickinson Hall were hushed, empty of the echoing laughter and stampeding footsteps that livened the dormitory during the day. A man crept slowly, silently forward, with his face half hidden by a black sweatshirt hood. His muscles were taut with alert caution. If someone spotted him, he was toast.

Up ahead, around a bend in the hall, a lone set

of footfalls padded on the carpet. Panicked, he flattened himself inside a door frame. From the corner of his eye he saw the woman pass by without turning onto his stretch of the hallway. She was stumbling in her high heels, as if she'd had one too many at whatever party she'd just come from. *Good—that means she's oblivious.* Soundlessly he let out his breath.

I should never have come here, he reproached himself for the hundredth time. *It was much too great a risk to take. If campus security catches me sneaking around here, I'm a dead man.*

All the same, he could scarcely afford *not* to take the chance. He no longer had the luxury of the Wakefields' ignorance. Steven had doubtless called the cops—after tonight, it would be near impossible to get to Jessica.

At last he reached the door of room 28, Dickinson Hall. He reached into the pocket of his black, hooded sweatshirt and drew out a white envelope, then stooped to slip it into the darkened wedge of space underneath the door.

Mission accomplished. He just prayed it would work.

And then, as quickly and silently as he had come, the black-clad figure made his way down the hall, slipped into the stairwell, opened the disabled emergency-exit door, and disappeared into the night.

Another day of wild, crazy, in-my-face blather, Elizabeth thought irritably as she stepped out of the elevator into the marble-paneled hotel lobby. *I don't know how much more excitement I can stand.*

All last night she'd tossed and turned, worrying about Jessica and feeling guilty about Mike. Now, running on four-odd hours of sleep, enduring eight more hours of a pep rally disguised as a press conference did not seem like an enticing prospect.

Elizabeth stopped at the front desk and tapped the counter bell to get the clerk's attention. "Excuse me, are there any messages for room 203?"

The clerk, a pointy-nosed woman with a supercilious expression, extracted a slip of paper from a labyrinth of numbered wooden slots.

"Oh yes, 203. Last night someone who said she was your sister called, but she refused to leave a message."

"What?" Elizabeth shrieked, her heartbeat like machine-gun fire. "Why didn't anyone put her through?"

The receptionist regarded Elizabeth with what appeared to be disdain. "According to our records, your—ahem—*companion* requested that we hold all calls."

Elizabeth's hands clenched into fists as tight as the knot in her stomach. *Mike, how could you?* she raged silently. But there was no point in getting annoyed with him now. "Can I use your phone?" she asked breathlessly.

The receptionist indicated the desk phone with a dismissive wave, then moved down the counter to assist another guest. Frantically Elizabeth punched in the digits of her home number.

Mrs. Wakefield answered on the second ring. Elizabeth cut short her greeting. "Mom, it's me. I got a message from Jess. Is everything OK?"

Her mother's voice was weary and relieved at once. "Oh, Liz, I'm so glad you called. Now, don't panic"—Elizabeth immediately started to panic—"but Jessica and Steven saw someone in the yard last night. Some weirdo was hiding behind a tree. Steven chased him off and called the cops, but Jess was a little . . . shaken."

"Oh my God!" Elizabeth saw several

passersby in the lobby turn to glare at her. She lowered her voice and cupped her hand over the mouthpiece. "Is everyone all right? Did they catch the guy?"

There was a pause on the other end of the line. "No," Mrs. Wakefield admitted finally. "But the cops promised to start making regular rounds by the house," she hastened to add. "Trust me, we're all fine. Jessica is safe."

Tears welled in Elizabeth's eyes. She leaned on the smooth marble countertop for support. *Jessica was in trouble, and I wasn't there!* Hideous possibilities churned in her mind. What if it wasn't just some random prowler? What if the thugs who killed Nick were after her sister now too? She felt sick just thinking about it.

"Liz? Are you there? Honey, everything's fine—really," Mrs. Wakefield assured her. "We'll see you this weekend. Jessica's really . . . looking forward to it."

"Me too," Elizabeth choked. "I've gotta go, Mom—give Jess my love." Nauseous waves of guilt crashed over her as Elizabeth replaced the phone receiver.

It took only a second to make the decision. She'd already taken enough notes to fudge a puff piece about the press conference. There was no way she could endure another whole day here when she was worried sick about her sister.

Decisively Elizabeth dinged the silver bell again

and met the receptionist's haughty glare. "I'd like to check out early, please."

"You're safe, Jessica. I'll never leave you." Nick's angel face radiated blinding golden light. Jessica was warmed by its glow, her soul suffused with rosy bliss, as they floated hand in hand through a boundless, brilliant blue sky. Jessica's ears sang with sweet, soundless music. Her heart soared with joy.

They were drifting through a billowy white cloud now. Jessica let go of Nick's hand and stretched out her arms, letting the soft, pearly clouds drift through her fingers like liquid satin. . . .

Then suddenly she was falling, plummeting through space. Nick's wide-eyed face receded faster, faster, until it was swallowed up into the clouds, lost to her forever. Jessica opened her mouth to scream, but no noise came out. She crashed to earth and realized all at once that she was sitting bolt upright in bed, her whole body damp with perspiration.

Yellow daylight filtered through her shades. Hopefully Jessica glanced toward the window, but it was closed.

"It was just a dream," she mumbled dully. The realization was heartbreaking. But that didn't mean she'd dreamed *all* those times she saw the angel, did it? His visits had seemed so real.

Then again, the flying dream had seemed real

too. And last night in the yard she'd been so groggy. What if she *had* just imagined the angel, like everyone said?

Waking, dreaming . . . it's all so confusing, Jessica thought bitterly. She was sleeping so much, nothing seemed certain anymore. Day blurred seamlessly into night. Right now the sun was shining, so it must be . . .

She glanced at her nightstand clock. 12:15 P.M., it read. Another day half consumed by sleep. Strange—she used to enjoy sleeping late. But now she felt like a prisoner of . . .

The pills.

Jessica focused on the small, white tablet sitting on her nightstand by a glass of water. *That's why I'm so woozy all the time,* she realized. She didn't want to feel that way anymore—it was so frustrating. Never having any strength . . . never knowing what was real . . .

An idea gleamed in her mind. There was a silver jewelry box on her nightstand, an engraved antique that had been her grandmother's. Jessica flipped the hinged lid and placed her morning pill carefully on the folds of red velvet lining. Yes. She'd do that with the next pill, and the next, and every pill after that. Maybe then her head would clear up. Maybe then she'd be able to tell once and for all if the angel was real . . . or if she'd really lost her mind.

* * *

151

The muffled sounds of whispering voices and creaking bedsprings were coming from behind the door of room 28, Dickinson Hall. Elizabeth frowned quizzically as she turned her key in the lock. As the door swung open, there was a loud clatter and even more violently squeaking springs. Elizabeth peered inside to see Nina and Bryan perched at opposite ends of the bed, unconvincingly pretending to study. Nina's dark hair was a disheveled mess, and Bryan's shirt was buttoned wrong and half untucked.

"I guess you two made up," Elizabeth said wryly. "Nina, your physics book is upside down."

"Huh? Oh." Nina inspected the textbook she was holding, then grinned sheepishly and tossed it aside. "OK, I'm busted. How could I stay mad at this big lunkhead for long?" She threw her arms around Bryan's neck.

"Lunkhead, huh?" Bryan pinned Nina playfully on the bed. "I guess that's better than the terms of endearment you were using yesterday. What were they again . . . scumbucket? Pig? 'That jerk who thinks with his—'"

"I'm sure Elizabeth doesn't want to hear our mushy pet names," Nina interrupted. "Hey, Liz, how come you're back early anyway? The Intense network wasn't intense enough for you?"

"Something like that." Elizabeth set down her bags, averting her eyes from the sight of Nina and Bryan making out on the bed. "I just remembered some stuff I had to take care of at home." She glanced over at the unblinking red light on the answering machine. "Did anyone call for me?"

Nina managed to pry her lips from Bryan's. "No, but someone slipped a note under the door late last night. It's on your desk. Looks like it's from a little kid or something."

"What would a kid be doing in our dorm late at night?" Oddly apprehensive, Elizabeth walked over to her desk and picked up the white envelope. Her name was written on it in a crude hand that could indeed have belonged to a child . . . or to someone writing left-handed to disguise his or her handwriting. Nervously Elizabeth slit open the envelope.

She pulled out the piece of paper inside and froze. Pasted on the white, loose-leaf sheet was a collage of newsprint letters that read simply, *Jessica needs you*.

"Liz, is everything OK?" Bryan asked. "You look like you just saw a ghost!"

"It's nothing." Elizabeth quickly folded up the note and stuffed it back into the envelope. She flashed a tight grin at Bryan and Nina. "Just . . . I think I'm going to leave for home a day early."

Elizabeth was laughing, her head tilted back. She had one arm around Todd and the other around Jessica. They were standing on the beach, all in their bathing suits—Elizabeth in her turquoise one-piece, Jessica in her hot pink bikini. The sun illuminated them from behind, burning golden-copper edges into the silhouettes of the twins' blond heads.

Sighing heavily, Jessica turned another page of her sister's photo album. Another picture of the twins embracing, their eyes crinkling with laughter, made her mouth tug in a sad smile. Wistfully Jessica traced the line of her sister's face through the plastic sleeve of the album. *We were all so happy then . . . so innocent,* she recalled. *And to think all that time I was counting the days until we left for college.* If only she'd known then that her high-school years would be the best of her life. She would never have left home, never let Elizabeth leave.

In spite of the morning and afternoon pills she'd skipped, Jessica sat slumped listlessly on Elizabeth's bed, exhausted. Missing her twin seemed to sap all the energy from her.

She stared at the picture of the twins with their arms wrapped tightly around each other. "I miss you so much, Liz," Jessica whispered. "I don't know how much longer I can go on without you."

Suddenly someone nearby cleared her throat. Jessica looked up and saw Elizabeth standing in the doorway.

For a moment Jessica couldn't move, speak, or breathe. Was she dreaming? She stared openmouthed at the vision that might or might not be her sister.

Then Elizabeth set down the duffel bag she

was carrying and folded her arms across her chest. "Jess," she said in the half-annoyed, half-amused tone that was unmistakably Elizabeth's, "what are you doing in my room?"

Tears sprang to Jessica's eyes at the same time that a grin stretched every muscle in her face. Wordlessly she bounded off the bed and tackled her sister in a giant bear hug. Elizabeth was solid and warm and real in her arms. Jessica never wanted to let go.

"Jess"—Elizabeth laughed through her tears—"I think you're starting to cut off the circulation in my arms." For close to five minutes her sister had been standing motionless, her arms clinging desperately to Elizabeth like a shipwreck survivor to a plank.

"Sorry," Jessica said in a childlike voice. "I'm just so happy to see you." She took a step back, and Elizabeth saw that there were tears in Jessica's eyes too.

"It's good to see you too," Elizabeth assured her, wiping away Jessica's tears with her sweater cuff.

She wanted to say more, to apologize for how long it had taken her to visit, but she was at a loss for how to put things. Her sister seemed so fragile—Elizabeth couldn't help fearing the damage one false move might do. Jessica's face was sunken and glassy-eyed, and she had easily dropped five, even ten pounds since Elizabeth last saw her.

"I'll tell you what," Elizabeth said brightly, squeezing Jessica's hands in hers. "Why don't you help me unpack, and then we'll do whatever you want—get a shake, rent some movies . . . or just hang around and talk. What do you say?"

A flicker of excitement struck Jessica's glazed-over eyes. "Just like old times," she whispered. "But Liz, I don't even care what we do just as long as we're together."

Elizabeth blinked back fresh tears. She had to keep her emotions under control so Jessica couldn't tell how worried she was. But it was so heartbreaking to see her twin this way. . . .

"OK, we can decide later," she said awkwardly, pushing all her concerns out of her mind. "Let me just put away some of this stuff."

Elizabeth unzipped her overnight bag and set to work unfolding piles of clothes. She turned toward the closet to hang up a dress and saw Jessica's wan figure standing stock-still, watching her. As Elizabeth bent over her luggage again, she became uncomfortably aware that Jessica's wide, puppy-dog eyes were following her every move.

Elizabeth straightened up and looked squarely at her sister. "Jess, is everything OK?"

Jessica nodded so hard, Elizabeth was afraid her sister's neck might snap. "Why . . . did I do something wrong, Liz?"

Elizabeth winced and enfolded her sister in a comforting hug. "No, of course not." As much as a part of Elizabeth was itching to shake her sister back to reality, she had to remember how disastrous all her attempts to intervene had been. All she had to do was keep Jessica company—and try not to do or say anything that might set her off.

"Jess, please," Elizabeth laughingly protested, putting up her hands as she leaned back against the pillows. "Really, I don't deserve this royal treatment."

Oh no—is she mad at me now? Jessica drew back her hands from her sister's blankets as if she'd been burned. "I'm sorry, Liz," she said hurriedly. "I just thought it would be fun to tuck you in. You know, like we were kids again."

Elizabeth smiled weakly. "OK, Jess. Sorry, I'm just tired. Go ahead."

Gleefully Jessica drew the bedclothes up around her sister's chin and tucked them lovingly under her shoulders. She patted the pillows on either side of Elizabeth's face and kissed her twin's forehead.

"Wasn't this a perfect day, Liz?" Jessica whispered. She'd spent every second with her twin, making up for lost time—looking through old photos, trying on old clothes, watching Elizabeth eat and swim in the pool and watch TV. If she didn't think her sister would mind, Jessica would stay to watch Elizabeth sleep. *Maybe I'll sneak in later to check on her,* she thought fondly.

"It was great hanging out with you, Jess," Elizabeth agreed, making Jessica beam. "I'm really exhausted now, though. I'll see you in the morning, OK?"

"OK, good night, Liz." Jessica planted a last quick kiss on her sister's cheek before turning out the light and heading to her room. She'd wanted to talk to her sister about the angel, but if Elizabeth was that tired, it could wait until tomorrow. She wanted her twin to concentrate fully on all the vitally important details.

Jessica closed her bedroom door behind her and did a little dance of excitement, enjoying the feeling of being alert, awake, alive. Since Elizabeth's return, Jessica had been infused with new strength. *And skipping the pills doesn't hurt,* she thought with sly satisfaction, plucking her bedtime tablet off the nightstand and dropping it into the jewelry box.

Just then she heard a low rumble outside. Jessica drew in her breath and ran to the window. She flung it open and craned her head out, searching for the angel. But all she saw was the ever present black-and-white police car, pulsing red and blue lights as it rounded the corner of Calico Drive.

Her shoulders slumped as she closed the window. Having Elizabeth back was unspeakably wonderful, but it wasn't the same as being with her angel.

Jessica sank to the floor and buried her face in her hands. *What if he's angry at me for letting my family chase him away?* she asked herself. *What if he's abandoned me forever, just like the real Nick did?*

Chapter
Twelve

"Hey, get out of here!"

Still rubbing the sleep from her eyes, Elizabeth looked up and saw Jessica standing in the opposite doorway of the bathroom in her pajamas, grinning widely. "Oh, sorry," she mumbled, her voice hoarse from sleep. "I'll come back."

"No, no! Stay!" Jessica scurried barefoot across the tiles, her robe flying behind her like a cape, and took hold of Elizabeth's elbow. "I was just playing—you know, fighting over the bathroom, just like old times! Isn't it great, being together like this?"

"Sure, yeah." Elizabeth was usually a morning person, but right now she felt groggy, disoriented by the strangeness of waking up at home under these circumstances. *And where did Jessica get all this energy anyway?* she wondered, blinking in amazement at her beaming sister. *I thought*

Mom and Dad said the sedatives were making her sluggish.

"And look, Liz." Jessica wheeled her sister around by the elbow and kicked Elizabeth's bathroom door shut. Elizabeth's old blue bathrobe was hanging from a hook on the door. "I arranged all your old stuff for you. See, towels, soaps, everything. Don't you feel right at home?"

Seeing the eager desire for approval in Jessica's eyes, Elizabeth forced a smile onto her face. "It's great, Jess. Thank you so much."

Jessica bounced up and down, clapping delightedly. "I knew it would make you happy, Liz! That's why I worked so hard making everything nice."

"Well, you did great, Jess." Elizabeth patted her twin's shoulder awkwardly. She was glad her presence seemed to revive Jessica's spirits, but all this constant doting was beginning to make her uncomfortable. And her sister's clingy attentiveness just served to remind Elizabeth that Jessica wasn't herself. The Jessica Wakefield who Elizabeth knew definitely did *not* let her life revolve around Elizabeth.

Elizabeth extracted her toothbrush from its holder and started brushing her teeth. In the mirror she could see Jessica parroting her motions with her own toothbrush, her reflection's eyes glancing sideways at Elizabeth all the while.

In the mirror Elizabeth's eyes met Jessica's,

and Jessica grinned through a mouthful of toothpaste. "Isn't this just like old times, Liz?" she asked again.

Elizabeth spat into the sink and smiled tiredly at her sister. "Exactly," she agreed. What else could she say? If she told Jessica she was creeping her out, she'd be crushed.

"Liz, there's something I really need to talk to you about," Jessica said, following her sister into the bedroom. Now was the time, she'd decided. She felt so close to Elizabeth—she couldn't hold back any longer.

Elizabeth sat down on her bed and regarded Jessica with an unreadable expression. "OK," she said slowly. "What is it, Jess?"

Jessica took a deep breath. She sat down on the bed beside Elizabeth and fumbled for her sister's hands. "It's about my guardian angel," she began. "See, I know everyone thinks he's not real, but I swear, he really is!"

"Jess, I—," Elizabeth began hesitantly.

"No, just let me explain," Jessica rushed on. "There was this TV show, and they were talking about him—I mean, about spirits watching over us from the dead. And then I saw the angel in a dream—only it *wasn't* a dream because the window was really open—and I swear, he had Nick's face!"

She paused for another gulp of air. Elizabeth

was staring wide-eyed at her. "And I just *know* it's Nick watching over me—I just *know* it is! Except after that night in the yard, I think we scared him off . . . and Liz, I'm so afraid he doesn't love me anymore. If he doesn't come back, I . . . I don't know what I'll do." A tear leaked from the corner of her eye. "You have to help me find him, Liz— he's all I've got left."

She squeezed Elizabeth's hands in hers and looked expectantly at her sister, holding her breath. Finally the truth was out.

"Jessica," Elizabeth said softly, gently, "I know you feel really strongly that there's a spirit protecting you."

"Yes!" This was good. Elizabeth was on her side. "He's so real, Liz—there's no way I could be imagining him."

Elizabeth's eyes were moist. "But Jess, maybe . . . maybe instead of believing he's real, the best thing to do would be to move forward . . . and accept that Nick's not coming back."

The words were like a steely slap in Jessica's face. She jerked her trembling, ice-cold hands out of her sister's grasp and clenched them into fists.

"How can you say that?" she shrieked. "You, of all people!" Jessica stared furiously into Elizabeth's wide eyes. "I *trusted* you, Liz. All this time I waited for you to come home because I thought you would believe me! I thought you'd be on my side!"

162

"Jess, I *am* on your side," Elizabeth said in a meek, small voice.

"No, you're not!" Jessica rose to her feet, propelled by anguish and rage. She jabbed an accusing finger in her sister's face. "You think I've gone insane, just like everyone else! But I'm *not* crazy! I'm *not!*" She let out a strangled moan of frustration and started pacing up and down the room, all her pent-up energy flooding out in a rush. "I'm just so alone," she wailed, throwing up her arms. "So lonely and sad all the time—and you don't even care!"

"I *do* care," Elizabeth insisted. She was twisting her hands anxiously in her lap and squirming as if she were under an interrogation lamp. "You've got to believe me, Jess; I care about you more than anything!"

"Then why did you abandon me when I needed you?" Jessica demanded. Her blood was boiling, her whole body trembling. Nothing mattered except making Elizabeth understand how badly Jessica was hurting inside. And if that meant hurting Elizabeth too, Jessica couldn't help herself.

She spat the words out contemptuously, hatefully. "First you're not around at all . . . then you show up, and all you can do is smash my hopes—just shatter the only thing that keeps me going!" Jessica glared venomously at Elizabeth, feeling her twin cower under her gaze. *"What kind of sister are you?"*

* * *

Danny propped his chin on his elbows and stared at the phone on his desk. It appeared to be a harmless enough object, but just looking at it, Danny felt as if he were riding a roller coaster of mixed emotions. So many agonizing what-ifs had swirled in his brain since Tom gave him Isabella's number. His insides were a bundle of raw nerves.

Do I really have the strength to face the rejection to end all rejections? he asked himself for the thousandth time.

But by now the excruciating limbo of not knowing seemed almost worse than any of the scenarios he'd imagined. He'd barely eaten or slept since Tom pressed the number into his hand. What did he have to lose?

The longer I put off calling, the longer I'll be trapped in what-if hell, Danny admitted to himself. *I might not get Isabella back, but at least I can get on with my life.* Finally he picked up the receiver; it seemed to weigh twenty pounds.

Danny painstakingly dialed the seemingly endless series of digits, which was probably equivalent to the cost of the call. A tinny, faraway bleat came through the line, as if the phone were ringing underwater. *"Guten Tag,"* a voice greeted him.

"Isabella Ricci?" Danny enunciated carefully, then waited, sweating bullets, through another series of chirps.

Finally a gruff male voice answered. "Hello?"

Danny's heart sank. The worst-case scenario—Mr. Ricci. The man who blamed Danny for his daughter's hospitalization, her amnesia, everything. "Yes, Isabella, please," he squeaked, trying feebly to disguise his voice.

"Who is this?" Mr. Ricci demanded suspiciously. "How did you get this number?"

At a loss for excuses, Danny gave up his pretense. "It's Danny Wyatt, Mr. Ricci," he said in his normal voice. "Please, I need to speak to Isabella. I just want to say hello."

"Can't you take a hint?" Mr. Ricci's voice was a low, controlled growl. "Why do you think we brought Isabella here? I don't want my daughter being reminded of anything or anyone at that horrible school!"

"Please, let me have just thirty seconds of her time," Danny begged, ignoring Mr. Ricci's harsh words. "What harm can that do?"

"She can't spare thirty seconds for any of the freaks and druggies who drove her to this," Mr. Ricci snapped. "She's with her family now—the people who care about her. We've got everything under control. Can't you just leave us alone?"

"But I care about her too," Danny insisted, swallowing his pride for Isabella's sake. "I just want to tell her I love her one last time. Please, Mr. Ricci, ten seconds!"

Suddenly a faint voice drifted through the white noise of the long-distance connection. A voice Danny would know anywhere, faint though it was.

"Dad?" Isabella asked weakly. "Is that Danny?"

Stay calm. Stay calm. Stay calm, Elizabeth repeated to herself like a mantra, trying hard not to flinch as Jessica went on ranting.

"You're so selfish!" As she spoke, Jessica jabbed an accusatory finger that pushed each and every one of Elizabeth's guilt buttons. "You wouldn't even take my calls! I could wither away and die for all you care!"

She doesn't know what she's saying, Elizabeth told herself, pressing her lips together in a flat line. *She's not herself. You're the rational one—you've got to stay in control.*

"You went away without even telling me." Each word was like a knife through Elizabeth's heart. "You knew how much I needed to talk to you, and you just avoided me! I thought something horrible must have happened to you! Do you know how scared I was? *Do you?*"

Elizabeth bit down on her lip so hard, she tasted blood. *Rational. Calm,* she told herself. *Anything I say will just set her off.*

"You know what, Liz?" Jessica stopped pacing and trained blazing eyes on her sister. Her face was flushed with rage, her mouth contorted into a snarl. "If I *have* gone crazy, it's *all your fault!*"

That was it. She couldn't take it anymore.

166

Rational or no, she didn't deserve this.

"Jess," she burst out, "it's *not* my fault! I can't do everything for you—you have to help yourself!" She knew she shouldn't be saying any of this, but she couldn't rein in the torrent of pent-up emotion. "I love you, but I have my *own* life—which happens to be falling apart at the moment since I've been such a wreck over you!"

Tears welled up in her eyes, blurring her vision. "I tried so hard, Jess; I really did," Elizabeth sobbed. "But you just kept pushing me away! I had to let go and let you live your own life . . . even though it's tearing me apart!" Fiercely she wiped the flood of tears on her face with her sleeve. "You have to get on with your life if you want to get better, Jess! Stop living in the past . . . and stop blaming me!"

Elizabeth trailed off, her explosive anger spent. Jessica was staring at her, shaking like a leaf, her face pale as death.

Oh no, Elizabeth thought. Her hand flew to her mouth in horror. *What have I done?*

"Izzy!" Danny cried desperately at the top of his lungs, gripping the phone receiver with both hands. "Izzy, it's me! Pick up—please pick up the phone!"

"Dad? Is that Danny?" Isabella's plaintive voice floated once more over the line. "Can I talk to him?"

167

"It's nobody, honey." Mr. Ricci's flat voice was muffled, as if he were cupping his hand over the mouthpiece. "Just a wrong number." *Click.*

Danny replaced the receiver with numb fingers, feeling as if his heart had been ripped from his chest and thrown, still beating, in his face. He buried his head in his hands and sat deathly still—for how long, he had no idea.

"Tombo, I know you meant well," he mumbled grimly as he sat slumped over his desk, "but I wish you'd never given me that number. In fact, right now . . . I wish I'd never been born."

All of a sudden the stale air of the dorm room seemed stifling. The crushing pain in his chest was unbearable. Every cell in his brain screamed *Isabella*.

And there was only one way to cure that. Danny jumped violently up, knocking his chair to the floor. Grabbing his jacket, he headed out the door in search of a bar—any bar. Anywhere he could drink Isabella off his mind.

Jessica stared blankly at Elizabeth, trying to absorb everything her twin had screamed at her. She couldn't process it all, but one thing was crystal clear: Elizabeth had talked to her like a real person, not like a china doll or a tiny child. It was as if the force of Elizabeth's angry words had shattered the glass wall that isolated Jessica from the rest of humanity.

Fresh tears of relief sprang to her eyes. Elizabeth *did* love her. Elizabeth loved her enough to be real with her.

"Oh, Liz," Jessica cried, throwing her arms around her twin. "I'm so sorry I said all those things. You're not a bad sister. I love you, Liz—I love you so much."

"I love you too, Jess." Elizabeth sniffled into her shoulder, her arms tightening around Jessica's waist. "And I'm so sorry I wasn't there when you needed me. I just didn't think you wanted me around."

"I do—I *need* you around," Jessica insisted. "Please, Liz, you've got to help me—I'm lost without you. I just want things to be the way they used to be. I promise, I'll do whatever you want me to do . . . and I swear I won't push you away again."

Sobbing and smiling at once, Elizabeth cupped Jessica's face in her hands. "That's all I needed to hear, Jess. It was killing me to keep my distance from you. From now on, I'm butting in whether you like it or not."

Chapter Thirteen

"Well, I guess this is good-bye," Mrs. Wakefield sang out as Elizabeth descended the stairs with her duffel bag. "Jessica, don't you want to come see your sister off?"

Jessica emerged from the kitchen, looking forlorn in a baggy T-shirt and sweats that swallowed up her gaunt frame. "You're leaving already?" Her face was crushed. "But I thought . . ."

Mr. and Mrs. Wakefield, hovering at the bottom of the stairs, exchanged anxious glances. Elizabeth did her best to ignore them—she understood now that pity was not what Jessica needed. She opened the front door and tossed her bag onto the stoop. "Mom, Dad, could Jess and I have a minute alone?"

She beckoned Jessica outside, and her twin followed, wide-eyed as a lost child. Together they sat down on the stoop. The afternoon was clear and

171

bright; with the sun lighting the neat green lawns, the block seemed peaceful, idyllic. It reminded Elizabeth of simpler, happier times . . . until she spotted the police cruiser rounding the corner.

Hoping Jessica hadn't spotted the car, Elizabeth focused straight into her twin's sea-colored eyes. "Listen, Jess, even though I won't be right here with you, I'll be thinking of you all the time. And figuring out some way to get you back on your feet."

"You mean like back with you, the way things used to be?" Jessica whispered incredulously. "Oh. But . . . but do you really think they'd let me come back?"

"If it's what you want, we'll find a way," Elizabeth promised more confidently than she felt. "But until then, don't give up, OK? Just stay strong, and we'll work something out—I swear."

Wide-eyed, Jessica nodded hard, as if she wanted to believe but couldn't quite bring herself to. Elizabeth felt a lump in her throat as she hugged her sister good-bye. Jessica's whole future—her whole *life* was riding on her now. And Elizabeth had no idea in the world how she was going to keep her promise to her.

"Hold still for a second." Todd reached across the diner booth, staring intently at a spot on Dana's chin. "You have some syrup on your face." He motioned as if he was going to swab it away with his napkin, then made a quick swipe with his tongue and sat back against the vinyl booth, grinning.

"Ewww!" Dana squealed, giggling. "Cooties!" She threw her napkin at him.

"I hate to break this to you," Todd said, spearing another forkful of his pancakes, "but my cooties have probably already crossbred with your cooties and founded a colony of mutant cooties."

Dana waggled her eyebrows. "If you're trying to turn me on, it's working." They burst into laughter and leaned across the tabletop to kiss.

Dana fell back against the booth with a sigh. She was wearing one of Todd's old basketball jerseys, her hair was pulled back in a messy ponytail, and she had no makeup on. Even so, she was the most breathtakingly beautiful woman Todd had ever seen.

"Todd, this has been the most perfect weekend. I wish it didn't have to end."

"Me too." Todd took a thoughtful sip of orange juice, mulling the prospect of dragging himself back and forth to classes, with memories of Gin-Yung lurking around every corner on campus. An idea occurred to him. "Well, why does it have to end?"

"Hmmm . . . maybe because it's Sunday? That's traditionally when the weekend ends."

Todd chucked her under the chin. "No, Ms. Sarcastic, I mean why don't we take our own personal long weekend? It'll be light for a few more hours. We could drive up the coast, rent a cheap room, then spend tomorrow sailing or swimming or—well, whatever. As long as we're together."

"That does sound wonderful," Dana agreed, her eyes dreamy. She shook her head, clearing the wistful look away, and cut a few squares from her Belgian waffle. "No, but I haven't even picked up my cello in days, and I have tons of reading piled up. Plus chemistry's tomorrow—my toughest class."

"So? I've got insane amounts of work to do too." Todd shrugged glibly. Somehow schoolwork just didn't seem to matter in Dana's intoxicating presence. The idea of being parted from her was far worse than the distant consequences of a day of missed classes.

It occurred to Todd that he also had an appointment with his therapist tomorrow—but he could always call her voice mail and cancel. Right now, with Dana, he couldn't think of any problems to discuss anyway.

"*That's* your argument? That it would be a dumb move for you too?" Dana's tone was incredulous, but there was a twinkle in her eye.

"Yeah, I guess." Todd reached across the scratched Formica tabletop and covered Dana's small hand with his broad palm. He gave her his most endearing grin. "Pretty convincing, isn't it?"

Dana's stern face relaxed into a mischievous smile. "Yeah, actually." She chuckled. "OK, you bad influence. Let's do it."

"Come on, Liz, admit it." Nina waved a carrot stick across the table at her friend. "You missed the SVU cafeteria food. I bet your mom's home-cooked meals have got nothing on this . . . what *is* this soup anyway?"

Elizabeth listlessly stirred her own bowl of brown, vegetable-flecked mush. "I'm not sure, but even if it was beluga caviar and truffles, I still wouldn't have an appetite."

"You hate caviar," Nina pointed out. "You always say you never understand why fish eggs are considered a delicacy."

"Oh. Right." Elizabeth dropped her spoon into the mush, where it remained disturbingly buoyant, and sighed heavily. "The point is, I'm just not hungry. I can't stop thinking about Jessica."

Nina reached across the table and gave Elizabeth's shoulders a comforting squeeze. "I'm sure you'll think of some way to help her out, Liz. I mean, it doesn't seem right that the school could just kick her out like that. Isn't there an appeals process or something?"

"I'm not sure," Elizabeth admitted, staring pensively into space. "Jessica said there was a hearing to discuss the plagiarism charges, but I'm sure in her condition, she didn't do a very good job of making a case for herself."

"Well, of course not—she wasn't in any state to deal with a hearing!" Nina exclaimed indignantly. "Wouldn't Jessica's psychological problems be grounds for an appeal?"

"It seems only fair to me," Elizabeth agreed, swirling a bread stick in her rapidly congealing soup. "But I'm not sure the administration would see it that way."

"There's got to be a case you can make," Nina persisted. "It just seems unfair to punish somebody for going through a rough patch emotionally."

Elizabeth nodded slowly, pondering Nina's words. She was silent for a minute, then let go of the bread stick and snapped her fingers. "Wait! I just thought of something! The Americans with Disabilities Act!"

"Disabilities?" Nina echoed, dropping an uneaten spoonful of soup back into her bowl. "Isn't that just for people with physical conditions?"

"Well, when I worked at WSVU with Tom, we did this story," Elizabeth explained, excitedly pushing her tray of food aside, "about students with disabilities and their rights on campus. We found out that the Americans with Disabilities Act extends to people with psychological problems, under certain circumstances." Elizabeth sighed in frustration and tore her paper napkin in half. "I wish I still had all that research again. It'll take days to track down all that information again, maybe weeks."

Nina looked puzzled. "Doesn't the station hold on to files from old stories?"

Elizabeth looked down at the napkin she was shredding in her lap. "Well, yeah, but they're over at the WSVU offices. The only person who'd even be able to track them down is Tom, so it's a moot point."

Nina's jaw dropped. "Are you serious? You would pass up a chance to help your sister because you'd have to deal with Tom?"

"I can't face him after all the horrible things he said to me!" Elizabeth felt her face flush, realizing how petty she sounded. "Besides, I can't just come crawling to him—he'd probably laugh in my face."

"He would *not*." Nina rapped on the table for emphasis. "Get over yourself, girlfriend! Tom's an adult, and so are you. If you just swallow your pride and explain that Jessica's future is on the line, I'm sure he'll help you out."

"*Ohhh*, why do you have to be right all the time?" Elizabeth groaned, smiling sheepishly at Nina. "No, honestly, thanks. You're a real friend. And Nina . . . I'm sorry I didn't open up to you sooner. I just couldn't. . . ." She trailed off, spreading her hands helplessly.

Nina grinned and waved her aside. "I know, I

know. You weren't ready to deal. But now that you're talking about it, don't you feel better already?"

"Actually, yes." Elizabeth felt her spine straighten, the weight on her shoulders lightening. Finally she was ready to put aside her guilt, her shame, and her stubbornness to help her sister. Finally she was ready to move forward. She just hoped Jessica was too.

Tom took a sip of coffee from his WSVU mug and made a face. It was after 8 P.M., and Tom was the only one left at the WSVU station office. The coffeepot had been heating since morning, and now the condensed black sludge was almost as bitter as Danny was over Isabella. *Almost*—which was part of the reason Tom was putting in long hours at the station. His roommate had been climbing the walls of the dorm room since Tom gave Danny Isabella's number.

I'll just stick around a few more minutes, Tom decided. *Lila* did *say she'd call me here to make a plan for the date.* Not that he was exactly eager to play Dream Date Tom to some high-school Barbie doll, but it would at least be nice to know when the ax was going to drop.

He had turned back to his computer keyboard and was adding the final touches to a hard-hitting story on campus library fines when a knock sounded on the door.

"Come on in; it's open." Tom wheeled his desk chair around to see possibly the last person on earth he had expected to encounter. "Liz?" he gasped. "What are you doing here?"

Elizabeth was hovering skittishly in the open doorway, like a bird about to fly away. In a white, cable-knit sweater and blue leggings, she looked soft, innocent, sweet. Tom longed to sweep her into his arms and hold her tight. He had to shake himself to focus on what she was saying. "Tom, I know you might not want to talk to me right now, but I need your help. It's about Jessica."

Tom narrowed his eyes warily. A part of him wanted to throw himself at Elizabeth's feet and promise her any kind of help she needed. But her showing up here out of the blue—with an agenda, no less—was just too suspicious. *Is this some ploy to get a scoop for the* Gazette? he wondered. *Is she just trying to mess with my head? Does she hate me enough to stoop to using her sister as part of some scheme?* "Jessica? What could I possibly do to help Jessica?"

Elizabeth hadn't budged from the doorway. "Well, remember that story we did on disabled students? How we did all that research on the Americans with Disabilities Act?"

"How could I forget?" Tom couldn't resist asking in a low voice. "We did some of our best work together on that story."

Elizabeth flushed an exquisite crimson to the

179

tips of her ears. Tom wondered if she was recalling what he was—the hours they'd spent kissing passionately on the office couch while they were supposed to be working on that story.

"Yes. Well. Um," Elizabeth stammered. "Anyway, I think Jessica's . . . condition might qualify legally as a disability. And with any luck, maybe I can use that to get her readmitted to SVU. But I need access to our research to put a case together."

Tom folded his arms guardedly across his chest. He couldn't help but feel touched by the sight of Ms. Obstinate herself laying down her arms for her sister's sake. But he had to steel his foolishly swelling heart against the possibility that Elizabeth had some ulterior motive. "So I guess you just want me to hand over the notes?" he asked a little more curtly than he'd intended.

Elizabeth took a tentative step into the station office. "Look, I know you don't trust me right now, but believe me, I wouldn't be here if I had anywhere else to turn." She clasped her hands together beseechingly, her aquamarine eyes searching his face. "I swear, all I want is to help Jess. If it'll make you more comfortable, you can watch me the whole time."

Watch you the whole time, huh? Tom contemplated the prospect of working side by side with Elizabeth, just like in the days when they were a couple. This might be his last chance to get back on her good side. Maybe going over one of their old stories would rekindle some old sparks. . . .

You're getting ahead of yourself, Watts, Tom cautioned himself. *First things first.* He got up and headed toward a row of filing cabinets by the wall.

"All right, Wakefield. As long as I'm keeping an eye on you, I might as well give you a hand." Tom yanked open a bottom drawer marked Archives and crouched down, leafing through the densely packed file folders. "Pull up a seat—this could take a while."

"Run that by me one more time?" Elizabeth scribbled furiously in her notebook, her mind racing to process everything Tom was saying.

Tom scanned the newspaper clipping he was holding. "It says that psychiatric conditions make up the largest percentage of disability claims, but they don't have a high rate of success. The tough part is defining what counts as discrimination based on mental disorders—it's trickier than with physical disabilities. You have to prove that somebody qualifies as disabled, *yet* that their disability doesn't prevent them from doing the job."

"That sounds like kind of a catch-22." Elizabeth set down her pencil and rubbed her tired eyes. They'd been going over the notes for almost two hours. "So would this cover school enrollment as well as employment?"

Tom frowned as he pored over the paper. Elizabeth realized suddenly how long it had been since they worked on a story together. She'd almost forgotten how sexy Tom looked when he was concentrating hard. His handsome face and muscular body were attractive enough, but his razor-sharp intelligence and inquisitive mind were what had always drawn Elizabeth irresistibly to Tom. They were both born journalists. And they worked so well together. . . .

"Liz? Are you listening? I said it looks like it does apply to schools too. And a testimonial letter from a family member or close friend will count as evidence."

Elizabeth shook herself out of her reverie. *Jessica—you're here to help Jessica,* she reminded herself sternly.

"So I'd have to argue that it was discriminatory to expel Jessica without taking her mental disorder into account," she mused. "It sounds like such a long shot. What if the school turns around and says that if Jessica's condition is that serious, she's not fit to attend SVU anyway?"

"Come on, Liz, don't sell yourself short," Tom said encouragingly. "You're such a convincing writer, you could persuade people in Alaska to buy snow. Besides, you and I have the *Gazette* and WSVU behind us, so you can always play the bad-press card."

"That's true—a sympathetic case like Jessica's could stir up major negative publicity," Elizabeth realized, brightening. She jotted some notes on her pad, struck with a rush of inspiration she hadn't felt since the last time she covered a story with Tom. "Thanks—this is a huge help."

"Anytime," Tom said in a low voice.

Elizabeth gazed up at Tom. Their eyes locked, and she saw the intense, undisguised longing in his expression. She swallowed hard, her mouth suddenly dry.

I guess he doesn't hate me as much as I thought, Elizabeth realized. *If he would actually be willing to use WSVU to help Jessica's case, he must really care.* She felt a surge of gratitude and had to restrain herself from jumping up to hug Tom.

Elizabeth cleared her throat. She could feel the way his entire body was at attention, focused on her. The air between them crackled. Her palms were clammy with anticipation; she pressed them against her cotton-clad thighs, fighting to steady her nerves. "Tom, I—"

Just then the moment was shattered by the sound of the phone ringing. "Who would be calling the station at this hour?" Elizabeth wondered aloud, startled.

"I have no idea," Tom said in a strangled voice. His eyes had darted to the phone. His face was turning a shade of red that suggested he did indeed know who was calling . . . and that he didn't want Elizabeth to find out.

*　　*　　*

"Well, aren't you going to answer it?" Elizabeth demanded as the phone shrilled for the fifth time.

Tom gulped. *Please don't let it be Lila*, he prayed as he picked up the phone. *Not now—not when Liz and I are getting along so well.* The last thing he needed was for Elizabeth to find out he was going out with some high-school senior. He willed his face to remain impassive, but he could tell from Elizabeth's narrowed eyes that she already suspected something was up.

"Hello?" he answered apprehensively, his heart in his throat. *Please, anyone but . . .*

"Tom, it's Lila! I'm sorry to call so late, but I didn't hear back from Chloe until just now."

Tom cringed. Lila's voice was so loud, he wanted to hold the phone away from his ear— except that would make it easier for Elizabeth to overhear. As it was, she could probably make out every word.

Tom turned his back to Elizabeth. "Uh-huh. That's fine," he said neutrally.

"Tom? Why do you sound so weird? You're not thinking of backing out of the date, are you? Remember, we had a deal!"

"Sure," Tom said through gritted teeth. With any luck, monosyllabic answers would keep Elizabeth from figuring out the situation. And yet he could feel her eyes boring into his back.

"Good. OK, so we have a reservation at the

Côte d'Argent for six-thirty tomorrow," Lila went on, ignoring his discomfort. "You might as well just meet us there. Dress is semiformal, of course. And bring your gold card."

What *gold card*? Tom wanted to snap. "Sounds good," he said noncommittally instead.

"All right, I'll see you then." There was an annoyed note in Lila's voice. "And Tom—I've been talking you up to Chloe. She's expecting a magical evening with a charming guy. So you better work on improving your conversational skills before tomorrow."

"Will do," Tom said with a short, forced little laugh. He hung up and let out his breath. *That didn't sound too incriminating, did it?* He turned slowly, hopefully, to face Elizabeth.

The expression on her face was withering. "Thanks for all your help, Tom," she said in a voice that could freeze molten lava. "Have fun on your 'magical evening.'"

"Elizabeth! Wait! Don't go—I can explain!"

"Don't bother, Tom." Elizabeth was halfway toward the glass doors of the station, slinging her backpack over her shoulder and shrugging on one arm of her cardigan at the same time. "It's none of my business who you're dating." *Although you certainly didn't waste any time,* she added bitterly to herself. *Are you already sleeping with this one too?*

She marched purposefully past the security

185

desk, pulling her other arm through her sweater. Tom followed, his clattering footsteps echoing noisily down the empty corridor. "I'm not *dating* anyone, I swear! It's just one blind date—a favor!"

Elizabeth pursed her lips and picked up her pace, tuning Tom out as he babbled some incoherent, implausible nonsense about doing Lila a favor for Danny's sake. And to think she was actually starting to let herself feel something for Tom again! Hadn't she learned that getting distracted by men was not what she needed right now? She'd come to WSVU for Jessica's sake—nothing more. Elizabeth wanted to kick herself, but she didn't want to give Tom Terrific the satisfaction.

"You've got to believe me, Liz!" Tom panted at her shoulder. "I don't even know this girl—and I'm not looking forward to meeting her! There's nobody but you. It's always been you, Liz!"

Elizabeth whirled and trained cold, furious eyes on him. "Save it, Tom. You really don't owe me any explanations. We're broken up, remember? It's over. You can do whatever you want."

She turned and resumed heading toward the doors, but not before she saw Tom's face crumple and his shoulders sink in defeat. After a second Elizabeth became almost eerily aware that hers were the only footsteps echoing in the lobby.

* * *

The sleek, black-and-white police cruiser glided slowly down Calico Drive, pausing briefly in front of the Wakefields' house. After a few seconds the engine growled again, and the car disappeared around a corner.

Down the block, the tip of a sweatshirt-hooded head was just barely discernible—if anyone had been there to see—through the windshield of a nondescript parked car.

He crouched down in the driver's seat until he was sure the cop car had gone by. Then, careful not to make any sudden movements, he lifted his head and glanced around the deserted street.

This is so damned frustrating. He felt like beating his head against the steering wheel. *Don't the cops have better things to do than patrol this block 24/7?* He knew time was running out, could feel it in his gut. Elizabeth was gone; Jessica was vulnerable, unprotected. But there was nothing he could do about it with the police breathing down his neck.

Up ahead, the light he knew was Jessica's blinked out. He longed to climb up into her room, to be alone with her in the darkness. But it would be a suicide mission—one noise, one cry from Jessica, and Ned Wakefield would have the cops back in a flash.

He started the engine and steered the car down Calico Drive, still hunched down low in the driver's seat. As he passed the Wakefield house, he blew Jessica a bittersweet kiss. *I'll find a way, my sweet,* he vowed silently.

Chapter Fourteen

"Did someone order a lawyer?" Steven asked as he pulled up a seat beside Elizabeth and Nina at Hill of Beans, the funky off-campus coffeehouse.

"Well, we couldn't afford one, so we had to settle for a lowly prelaw student," Elizabeth quipped. Lifting off the edge of a leopard-print velour stool, she gave her older brother a quick peck on the cheek. She sat back down and tore a sheet off her yellow legal pad. "Here's the letter we're drafting to the dean, vouching for Jessica's mental state at the time of the hearing." She slid the paper across the little round table to Steven. "I want your expert legal opinion. Let me know if you spot any loopholes in my argument."

Nina took a sip of her iced cappuccino and leaned back in an overstuffed, purple velvet antique armchair. "Hey, Steven, what do you think of this angle? I was telling Liz we should threaten to sue the school for negligence because they put Jess through this whole process without even picking up on the fact that she wasn't well."

Steven nodded as he scanned the dense lines of Elizabeth's handwriting. Elizabeth watched him a little nervously as she drank her iced tea. "You could say that putting Jess through a hearing exacerbated her distress after Nick's death. I don't think a case like that would ever get to trial, of course, but it's a good card to play from a PR perspective."

"Good point," Nina agreed. "I doubt driving a bereaved girlfriend to a nervous breakdown would be good for the school's image."

"Especially since Nick's picture was all over the papers and local news." Hunkered forward on her stool, Elizabeth busily jotted some notes on her pad. "I can't even count how many times the press called him a hero. The administration would really come off looking like ogres if word got out that they expelled his girlfriend during the depths of her depression."

Steven handed the letter back to Elizabeth. "I think this looks good, Liz. Just make sure you downplay the issue of the plagiarism itself. From a legal point of view, you should be stressing the fact that it doesn't matter what Jess did wrong—the point is she didn't get a fair trial."

"And therefore the ruling should be thrown

out," Elizabeth concluded, feeling a surge of optimism as she scrawled some more notes on the letter. The case was really starting to come together.

"Exactly," Steven confirmed. "Great work, Liz. I'm proud of you—this is a great thing you're doing for Jess." He beamed at her. "If there's anything else I can do to help, just let me know."

Elizabeth set down her pen, shook out her cramped fingers, and smiled up at her brother. "Thanks, Steven. And you too, Nina. I don't think I could face taking on the school without your support."

"Oh, come on." Nina draped an arm across Elizabeth's shoulders. "We both know you'd be championing truth and justice no matter what—right, Steven?"

"Of course." Steven reached over and rubbed Elizabeth's head affectionately with his knuckles. "Liz, you really should get a secret identity and a cool cape or something."

"Very funny." Elizabeth rolled her eyes, but she had a warm feeling inside. With her brother and her best friend by her side, she felt strong and confident. She was even daring to believe that she might just be capable of overcoming the odds—and helping Jessica get her life back.

"Danno, can you toss me that cologne?" Tom asked without turning away from the mirror, where he was running his fingers through his slicked-back hair.

Danny rolled over on his bed, willing himself to ignore the vaguely seasick sensation in his stomach—the result of last night's binge—and grabbed a square bottle of musk from Tom's nightstand. He stared for a second at his roommate's elegant, neatly pressed black suit and fought the urge to throw the bottle at Tom's head. *How can it be so easy for him to rebound from Elizabeth?* Danny wondered bitterly. *I couldn't even stand to think about taking out another girl right now. Maybe in . . . oh, I don't know—five years?*

"Heads up," Danny said a little abruptly, tossing the bottle.

"Thanks, man." Tom turned, caught it deftly, and spritzed the scent on the back of his neck. "Ugh—does this stuff reek, or is it me?"

"No, it's fine." Sprawled on his bed, Danny watched resentfully in the mirror as Tom slapped cologne onto his freshly shaved cheeks.

"I guess it's just been a while since I did the whole-nine-yards fancy date thing." Still gazing into the mirror, Tom straightened his maroon-dotted gold silk tie. "It feels weird to be going to all this trouble for somebody who isn't Elizabeth. It's like, why bother, you know?"

Danny gritted his teeth, biting back a sarcastic retort. Tom always seemed so together, so emotionless. Sure, the guy *claimed* he was hurting inside, but he sure didn't look it. He'd been whining about being strong-armed into this date with some rich chick for days—tough life! Meanwhile Danny's life was in ruins, thanks to his butting in . . . and Tom was totally oblivious. If anything, he was probably patting himself on the back.

Tom turned and spread out his arms. "So, do I look studly or what?"

Danny grunted, unable to muster up a civil response. When he looked at Tom, he didn't see his best friend—he saw the guy who'd blithely handed Danny the sword to open up all his Isabella-induced wounds.

Tom dropped his arms to his sides, looking crestfallen. "Hey, Danny, is there anything you want to talk about? You've seemed kind of down lately. If you don't mind me asking, did you ever end up calling Isabella?"

The dorm room lurched. Danny sat up straight, staving off an attack of nausea. Tensely he ran his fingers over his closely cropped hair.

"No, man," he said finally. "I just haven't gotten up the nerve yet."

Tom was watching him with his infuriating probing-journalist look, as if he were about to fire off a follow-up question. Danny wasn't about to give him the chance. The room felt oppressive; he got to his feet.

"I'm going to head to . . . the library," Danny said as he shrugged on his jacket.

"Without any books?" Danny heard Tom call as he strode out into the hallway. But Danny didn't bother to fish for an excuse. He'd already lied about calling Isabella; another fib wouldn't hurt.

Elizabeth shifted her weight from one tired leg to the other and checked her watch for the thousandth time in two hours. It was after 6 P.M.— Dean Nealy's office hours had ended over an hour ago. So why was the imposing oak-paneled door to his office still resolutely closed?

She slumped against the wall and sighed. The secretary, a gray-haired man in an impeccably pressed suit, looked up from his computer monitor. "Are you sure you wouldn't like to come back tomorrow? The dean has a reception for prospective parents tonight. I'm sure he'll be dashing out the door." The secretary flipped through a calendar on the desk. "Oooh, sorry, tomorrow's jam-packed too. It looks like I could squeeze you in . . . a week from Friday?"

Elizabeth set her jaw and straightened her spine. "I'll wait. This is urgent."

The secretary raised his eyebrows slightly to suggest he considered Elizabeth a hopeless case. "Suit yourself." He resumed typing.

Finally the dean, a balding man in a charcoal

suit, emerged from the office with his head down like a convict ducking a crowd of reporters. Briefcase in hand, he strode out of the reception area.

"Dean Nealy!" Clutching her sheaf of papers to her chest, Elizabeth hurried after him into the corridor. She wove through several students to catch up with the dean and tapped him on the shoulder. "My name is Elizabeth Wakefield, and I came to see you on behalf of my sis—"

He jerked around and brushed away the spot where she had touched him, as if a fly had landed there. "I'm sorry, but I'm running late to an important function. You'll have to set up an appointment with my assistant." The dean lowered his head and continued stalking down the hall.

"Please, Dean Nealy, this will just take a minute of your time." Elizabeth scurried after him, holding out the crisp, white envelope that contained her letter. "Or if you could just read this and get back to me . . ."

The dean, not slowing his pace, showed no sign that he heard her. Elizabeth paused and was nearly knocked over by a burly jock barreling past her. Seething, she crumpled the envelope in her fist.

"Fine," she called out loud enough for passing students all the way down the hall to hear. "If you won't talk to me, I guess you can read all about the charges of discrimination against disabled students in the *Gazette*—or watch the report on WSVU."

The dean froze in his tracks. Encouraged, Elizabeth went on, "Or maybe I should just tag along to the prospective parents' reception and tell *them* all about it."

"All right, all right, you've got my attention. Just keep your voice down." In a flash Dean Nealy had turned and was hustling Elizabeth into his office. "Make it quick."

His face beet red, the dean slammed the oak-paneled door shut behind them. Elizabeth couldn't suppress a satisfied smirk as she smoothed the wrinkled envelope and handed it over to him.

The shrill, hollow ringing in Jessica's ear sounded like mournful cries—like the ones she'd unleashed after Nick's funeral. Jessica gripped the phone receiver helplessly, as if it were a life preserver that was anchored to nothing. Why wouldn't Elizabeth pick up?

A terrible sense of emptiness overwhelmed her. This was all wrong. Elizabeth had said she would be there for her, even when she was away . . . but she wasn't.

A click cut short the rings, and then came the lifeless machine voice. *"Hi, we're not here right now—"*

Jessica hung up and hit redial. *Be there*, she prayed as the jangling sounded once more in her

196

ear. *Be there for me, Liz—like you promised!*

More ringing, then the soulless recorded voice. Jessica thought of leaving a message, but her throat had closed up. She slammed down the receiver with a strangled gasp of frustration.

Jessica paced frantically around her room, trying desperately to outrun the shadows that threatened to drag her down. Her palms were damp. Her heart was ricocheting back and forth in her rib cage.

"She's left me again," Jessica whispered to the achingly lonely room. Elizabeth had vowed things would be different, but now she was slipping away again. Jessica was alone, just like before. Her twin's promises seemed to withdraw into the distant recesses of Jessica's mind.

Maybe Elizabeth never even said all those nice things, Jessica realized. She was shaking; she felt cold all over, as if she was burning up with a fever. *Maybe I only imagined them because I wanted to believe them—just like with the angel.*

The angel. He'd abandoned her too. If he'd ever been there with her in the first place. She wasn't sure anymore. If Elizabeth could disappear, her promises vanishing into thin air like tissue paper in fire, then nothing was certain—except the crushing pain of her loneliness. *That* she couldn't possibly be imagining.

Jessica threw herself facedown onto her bed, grasping fistfuls of blankets in anguish. For a fleeting, beautiful time, she'd begun to hope that things could be different. That Elizabeth was on her side.

But without her twin, Jessica was cut off from the rest of the world, trapped here in her old room where time stood still. She would never get her old life back, never have anything to fill her days but the sorrow of missing Nick and Elizabeth . . . and the angel.

The setting sun blazed a broad band of fiery red across the golden sky. Dana and Todd walked hand in hand along the beach. Swinging her strappy sandals in her other hand, Dana shivered as the cool surf lapped at her bare feet.

Todd moved closer to her. "Are you cold, babe? Do you want to head back to the inn?"

Dana was a little chilly in her clingy, white spaghetti-strap top and short denim cutoffs, but she shook her head firmly. "Not yet. I'm not ready for this perfect day to end." Already she was savoring the sweet memories of their ride on the rented sailboat; their lunch at the quaint, picturesque garden restaurant . . . and their night together at the cozy, rustic bed-and-breakfast.

She sighed contentedly, noticing how strong and protective Todd's broad shoulders looked against the dusky sky. "This is the life, Todd—just you and me, far away from civilization." Dana had always loved to be where the action was, loved crowds and noise and excitement. But when she was with Todd, she felt so safe, so cared for, so complete that nothing else mattered. She couldn't imagine anything she would rather do than be with him.

Todd pointed out to the ocean, a pair of sneakers dangling from his hand. Dana followed his gaze to a faint swell of land on the horizon line. "Maybe if we wade out a little farther, we'll be swept out to sea and marooned on that island. I'd love to see you wearing nothing but palm fronds."

"I can see it now." Dana giggled. "The Swiss Family Wilkins." The spray of the cool sea air on her skin didn't matter; basking in the fact that Todd loved her as much she loved him, she felt warm all over. Dana grinned up at Todd and elbowed him in the ribs. "We'll have a very traditional marriage. I'll stay home and decorate the hut with seashells while you go out and hunt for coconuts. What do you say—should we elope to Tahiti, Todd? . . . Todd?"

Suddenly she sensed his body stiffening beside her and realized that his hand had gone limp in hers. She stared into Todd's face and saw that his expression had gone blank, then . . . twisted somehow. Dana's heart contorted wildly.

"Todd?" she cried anxiously, stopping in her tracks on the sand. "What's up? Did I do something wrong?"

Todd's lips took several seconds forming the

words before he managed to spit them out of his mouth. "Did I just hear you say . . . *marriage?*"

"I had the *worst* day today." Lila sighed, lifting a goblet of white wine to her lips. Candlelight twinkled off the wineglass stem. "First of all, my manicurist kept me waiting for at *least* twenty minutes."

Tom inadvertently took a rather inelegant slug of his wine. His eyes were starting to glaze over as he listened to Lila's shallow, self-absorbed monologue. His neck itched in the starched collar of his dress shirt, and his suit jacket was unbearably warm in the stuffy air of the upscale restaurant. As delicious as the escargot appetizer was, Tom would rather have been home in a T-shirt, scarfing cold leftover pizza.

"So then of course I was running late for my appointment with my trainer, and he made me do extra ab work just to get back at me," Lila went on. "And *then,* would you believe, I raced to the salon *only* to find that my regular stylist, Frédérique, ate some bad sushi and called in sick! So I got stuck with some incompetent clown." With a martyred sigh, she patted her flawless, complex updo.

Next to her Bruce shook his head. "Ugh," he said contemptuously. "It's ridiculous how hard it is to get decent service, even when you pay through the nose."

Glancing sideways, Tom saw Chloe Murphy give Lila a noncommittal nod of sympathy. Chloe was strikingly pretty, with auburn hair that fell in loose waves to her shoulders and ice blue eyes with long, fringed lashes. Her ivory skin glowed in the flickering candlelight. Her pale green sheath showed off her slim curves without being too flashy.

But so far she hadn't demonstrated much in the way of personality. After exchanging pleasantries, Chloe had mostly smiled politely and listened glassy-eyed to Lila's tales of trauma. Obviously she was just as vacuous as Lila and Bruce.

If only I were here with Elizabeth, Tom couldn't help thinking miserably. He took in the flower arrangements on the tables, the glittering chandeliers, the soft tinkling of violin music.

Tom was astonished to register that Lila was still droning on. "But the day wasn't a total waste. I did pick up some fabulous new skin-care products at the salon. They have this toner with beta . . . beta something—this brand-new scientific formula that exfoliates and—"

"Do you mean beta-keratonin?" Chloe interrupted. "I've been hearing a lot about that stuff."

Great, now she's going to share all her *beauty secrets.* Tom despondently buttered a warm roll. *Will this night never end?* They hadn't even ordered entrées yet, and already all this talk of exfoliating was making him want to claw his own face off.

"Yes, that's it," Lila said eagerly. "Have you tried it? Doesn't it make your skin tingle?"

"That tingle might be chemicals eating away at your skin," Chloe said gravely. "I've been following this story in *The New York Times*. The FDA is investigating the company that makes the product. I really wouldn't use it if I were you."

Tom perked up unexpectedly. *The New York Times*? Maybe Chloe wasn't quite as brain-dead as he had assumed. He turned to her with new interest. "Come to think if it, I think I read something about that in the *Times* too. Didn't a group of women file a class-action suit against the manufacturers?"

Chloe nodded eagerly, her crystal blue eyes sparkling with intelligence. "They're claiming the product causes permanent skin damage. It's actually really similar to a case I was reading about in my feminist-law class."

"You're taking feminist law in high school?" Tom asked in surprise. This was the last thing he had expected from one of Lila's friends, especially a seventeen-year-old.

Chloe shrugged modestly and took a dainty sip of her ice water. "Well, I take a couple of college courses at night. I'm hoping to rack up enough credits to finish college in three years so I can take a year off before grad school to go backpacking around Europe. Anyway, about this case . . ."

Tom listened as Chloe eloquently explained the legal precedent for the skin-cream lawsuit, blown away by how unexpectedly well-spoken and well-informed she was. Lila looked miffed that she'd lost the spotlight, and Bruce just looked bored, but Tom couldn't care less. All of a sudden he had noticed that Chloe's lovely features were even more attractive when she was animated. Maybe the night wouldn't be such an excruciating waste of time after all.

Dean Nealy looked up from Elizabeth's letter with a grave face. He set down his reading glasses on the huge, marble-top desk and rubbed the bridge of his nose. "You've made some very serious charges here, Ms. Wakefield. Discrimination, negligence, lack of due process . . . Are you prepared to put your sister through the added strain of more hearings, more questions?"

Across the desk Elizabeth perched on a chair, with her hands folded primly in her lap to keep them from shaking. "I'm hoping it won't come to that," she said evenly, in spite of the butterflies that had formed a conga line in her stomach. "I'm sure you agree that it would be better for everyone if we could handle this quietly. I doubt it would reflect well on the school if word got out that the tragic death of a heroic cop resulted in his devastated girlfriend being expelled."

The dean pursed his lips and regarded Elizabeth

for a moment, his cheeks twitching. "And how exactly do you propose we *handle* this?"

"I think the letter proves that Jessica's expulsion should be overturned." Elizabeth struggled to maintain her confidence, meeting the dean's steely gaze with a poker face. "All my sister needs is a little time to get back on her feet, with counseling. I'm sure that she'll be happy to make up all her missed course work—extra credit, summer school, whatever it takes."

"Plagiarism is a very serious charge, Ms. Wakefield," the dean said severely. "Sweet Valley University has an academic reputation to uphold."

"Believe me, my sister's psychiatrist can vouch for the fact that she was in no condition to judge what was plagiarism," Elizabeth insisted. "Please, Dean Nealy—my sister never meant to do anything wrong. She's just been through a terrible time. Won't you give her another chance?"

With each second of the dean's stony silence Elizabeth's heart sank another inch. *This really is Jessica's last chance,* she realized. She was too fragile to withstand the scrutiny of more doctors, more hearings, or lots of publicity. What if the dean called Elizabeth's bluff?

Then Dean Nealy's eyes softened. He sighed and pushed back his chair. "Ms. Wakefield, I really must be getting to my reception," he said in a not unkindly tone. "But why don't you set up a meeting with my secretary, and we'll discuss your sister's situation further? I'm sure we can work something out."

Jessica leaned her head against her windowpane and listlessly traced the outline of a winged figure on the glass. The bloodred sky had given way to a deep blue twilight. The shadows edged ever closer, whispering evil things. *He's not coming for you. He's abandoned you!* But still Jessica hadn't budged from her silent vigil by the windowsill.

She had nothing else to do with herself anyway. Since she'd stopped sleeping the days away, the hours crawled painfully by. Nobody was there to keep her company. Her parents could barely look at her, let alone talk to her. Elizabeth had warded her off with empty promises, then forgotten her entirely. The idea that she could actually help Jessica was a distant, abstract notion. And as for the angel . . .

He's never coming back, the shadows hissed. *He lived in the pills all along.*

"No, it can't be," Jessica whispered. "I saw him before the pills . . . didn't I?" All of a sudden she couldn't remember. Everything in the past was a blur. There was only pain, only the dark hole full of shadows.

Jessica's heart was sinking. With an effort she lifted her head and turned away from the window. Her eyes fell on the silver jewelry box on her nightstand. Slowly, as if she were mesmerized, she went over to her bed and picked up the box.

She'd stopped taking the pills because she needed an answer. And now she had her answer—even if it wasn't the one she wanted. *The pills do make the angel appear,* she admitted to herself, feeling as if her heart had been torn into a million pieces. *The angel was only in my dreams.*

Jessica opened the jewelry box and sank down onto her bed, staring at the small heap of pills in wonderment. Did the angel really live in those tiny little pills? There were so many saved up already.

Her mind was spinning, treading in circles. *Maybe I should start taking them again,* she mused. *Maybe they would bring him back.*

But that didn't seem like enough. She couldn't go on like this much longer—so alone all the time, just killing time with sleep and pining for her angel. *What kind of life would that be?* Jessica asked herself bitterly. *Just living for my dreams . . .*

Then she had a better idea.

If my dreams are better than my real life, maybe I should just live in my dreams.

Jessica felt her heart begin to beat faster as the thought took root in her mind. Maybe if she took all the pills at once, she would be with her angel forever.

"Another round." Danny slammed down his empty shot glass on the oily, stained, dark wooden surface of the bar. The bartender, whose hair and skin looked only slightly less greasy than the bar itself, wordlessly poured tequila into the glass and shuffled away.

Danny slapped a few wrinkled bills on the bar, half watching the few haggard men who were slumped over their drinks. Normally he wouldn't set foot in a dive like this, but right now he didn't care about his surroundings. *It's not like I'm here to have a good time,* he thought bitterly as he raised the glass to his lips. *All I care about is getting so wasted that I forget Isabella Ricci ever existed.*

He tossed back his head and slugged the shot. It tasted like gasoline in his mouth, burned like fire down his throat, and settled like acid into the lining of his stomach. But to Danny the awful sensations were a welcome relief. At least for a second, he had a distraction from the pain of losing Isabella.

But as soon as the glass touched the bar, the ache engulfed him again. He could still hear her plaintive voice echoing in his mind. Calling his name.

Danny clenched his fists, fighting the urge to punch a hole in the already cracked wall. There was only one possible outlet for his frustrated energy.

"I'll take another shot," Danny barked, signaling the bartender. He could feel his movements loosening, becoming less precise with each drink.

But his head was still crystal clear, the sound of Isabella's voice as acute as a thousand pinpricks.

As the bartender poured, a gravelly voice sounded at Danny's elbow. "You're really knocking those back, huh?"

Danny turned and saw a scruffy, unshaven guy in a baseball cap who could have been anywhere from twenty-eight to thirty-five. Danny eyed him warily. "I guess."

"College man, huh?" The guy looked Danny up and down, his eyes lingering on Danny's SVU jacket. "So whatcha doing in a place like this?"

Danny burst out in a coughing fit as the tequila tingled in his throat. "Forgetting my troubles," he wheezed. "Women troubles, that is."

"Say no more." The man raised his glass in the air, and Danny noticed how dirty his fingernails were. "Nothing helps you get over a woman like booze."

Danny grimaced, and not just from the tequila aftertaste. "I wish."

"I can't believe what passes for a rack of lamb outside Europe," Bruce declared as he slipped a shimmering, peach, silk wrap over Lila's slender shoulders. "I mean, that restaurant was actually one of the *better* places around here—although that foie gras was *foul*."

"And my duck l'orange was fatty," Lila pouted as they walked toward the curb outside the restaurant.

"Honestly, Bruce, I don't know how we stand these little provincial dives. Sometimes I wish I'd never even *tasted* the food in Paris."

"My heart bleeds for you," Tom muttered under his breath. Nothing was ever good enough for Lila and Bruce—the food, the wine, the service. They hadn't stopped nitpicking all night. Luckily Tom and Chloe had kept up a lively discussion about politics, which had distracted Tom from the urge to lunge across the table and strangle Bruce and Lila with their napkins.

"I thought everything was excellent," Chloe spoke up. Tom saw that her face was lit with a smile, her ivory skin luminous in the night air.

Chloe might have the same pedigree as Lila and Bruce, but she's totally down-to-earth, Tom thought approvingly. She hadn't joined in their grousing at all—in fact, at one point she'd gently intervened to defend a waiter whom Lila and Bruce were dressing down.

A valet had pulled Bruce's car up to the curb. "So, what say we go by the country club for a nightcap?" Bruce suggested, holding out a hand for his keys. "Chloe, you and Watts can be our guests for the evening."

"It's a *très* exclusive club, Chlo," Lila added. "Come check it out—I just know you'll want to join if you end up coming to SVU."

Tom groaned inwardly at the prospect of a late night at Snooty Central. He glanced nervously over at Chloe. Her delicate features were crunched into a yawn, a dainty hand covering her open mouth.

"You know, I'm really exhausted," Chloe said in a thick, sleepy voice. "And I have to get up early for my flight tomorrow. Thanks for everything, Lila, but I think I should call it a night."

"I'll drive you back to your hotel, Chloe," Tom volunteered quickly, seeing his car pull up behind Bruce's. He shooed Lila and Bruce into Bruce's Porsche. "You two go ahead to the club. No, really, we're fine."

Lila hugged Chloe good-bye and made her promise to call soon while Tom beat a hasty retreat into the driver's seat of his car. After a minute Chloe plopped down into the passenger seat. Forcefully she slammed her door shut, sighing hugely.

"Thanks for a great dinner, Tom." The drowsy tone had gone out of Chloe's voice. "I hope you don't mind skipping the country club."

"Are you kidding?" Tom inadvertently jerked the steering wheel to veer away from Bruce's Porsche, alarmed at the thought that Chloe might change her mind. "I mean, I'm pretty tired too."

"Oh, I'm not tired." Chloe giggled as she extracted a rhinestone barrette from her hair and set it on the dashboard. "I'm just not into the whole country-club scene. The people I hang out with talk about what bands they're into, not what stocks and bonds they invest in."

"I hear you." Tom chuckled. He was liking Chloe more by the minute. "Although, you know, it does get pretty wild and crazy when they start getting into mutual funds."

"Be still, my heart!" Chloe combed her slender fingers through her auburn waves and groaned. "You know, Lila's got a lot of great qualities and everything, but tonight I didn't think I could take another minute of her and Bruce. They're kind of full of themselves, you know?"

"I definitely wouldn't call them *humble*," Tom said diplomatically as he turned onto the freeway.

"I mean, I feel *guilty* that I've had so many advantages in life while other people have to struggle," Chloe went on. "But they act like their money makes them *better* than everyone else. That's kind of a screwed-up priority system, if you ask me."

"I couldn't have said it better myself." Tom was trying to keep his eyes on the road, but they kept darting toward Chloe's animated face like a moth to a halogen lamp. He hadn't met a girl who was not only beautiful, but smart, mature, and grounded since . . . *Since Elizabeth*, he realized with a little start.

"By the way, can I reimburse you for dinner?" Chloe asked casually. "That pretentious place must've been absurdly overpriced."

"No, don't be silly!" Tom was flabbergasted that she would even offer such a thing. "Please, it was my pleasure. It's been a lot of fun getting to know you." He turned to give her a lingering look that would have sent his driver's-ed teacher into conniptions.

"Well, at least let me buy you a cup of coffee or something," Chloe insisted. "C'mon, Tom, the night is young—and it's my last night in Sweet Valley."

Tom turned right. "I know a great place to get coffee around here." From the corner of his eye he saw Chloe grin. Tom was astonished at how unexpectedly well this was going.

Why not? he asked himself. He deserved to have a little fun. It wasn't as if Elizabeth was coming back to him, no matter what he did. She'd said it herself: It was about time Tom realized he didn't have a girlfriend anymore.

"Good-bye, Mom. Good-bye, Dad," Jessica murmured as she floated through the hallway, her fingertips caressing the cold glass over the photographs while her other hand clutched the jewelry box full of pills. Her parents looked so young, so beautiful. Her mother was a vision in her flowing, gauzy white wedding dress, illuminated by golden light. *I'll be beautiful and glowing like that when I'm with my angel,* Jessica realized, feeling warm all over.

212

"Good-bye, Steven." As she descended the stairs, Jessica smiled tenderly at the frame that held a photo of her baby-faced big brother at his high-school graduation. Her heart was swelling with love for her family. Now that she knew she was going to be with Nick, a peaceful glow of calm had come over her. Everything was heavenly and lovely.

She stopped at the bottom of the stairs and gazed fondly at a picture of herself and her twin. *Elizabeth . . . I've got to talk to her one last time.* Jessica drifted to the phone, her body lighter than air.

Elizabeth wasn't there. *That's all right,* Jessica thought serenely. *I'll be all right without her. Nick will take care of me now.*

The beep chimed in her ears. "Liz, it's me. I'm just calling to say good-bye." She wished her sister could see the smile on her face, could share Jessica's happiness. "I'm going to be with my angel now. Don't worry about me—everything is fine. And Liz . . . I forgive you. I understand."

She put down the phone and wandered away. Out the door, through the yard, down the street. She was floating in a blissful haze.

Up ahead she could see a dense cluster of trees, like an enchanted forest in a fairy tale. *That's the place,* she realized at once. The angel would find her there—she could feel it.

Drawn irresistibly, Jessica made her way

213

through the trees into a clearing. She saw a swing set, its swings hanging empty in the night air; a shiny, battered slide; the looming, spiderlike metal coils of a jungle gym. It all seemed familiar, like something she had seen a long time ago. She could almost see herself and Elizabeth as little girls, clambering up the slide, pushing each other in the swings.

I'm surrounded by happy memories, Jessica thought, a wellspring of joy gurgling up inside her. It was a perfect way to say good-bye to her old life . . . before she started her new, ecstatic existence with the angel.

Jessica sat down on a bench, shivering a little in the gauzy white dress she'd chosen just for the occasion. She unfurled her hands, which had been clasped rigor-mortis tight around the little jewelry box. Inside, the pills gleamed like small pearls.

Slowly Jessica lifted the first one to her mouth. It went down easily, the chalky scrape against her throat hardly registering. She reached for a second pill. She reached for a third.

Chapter
Fifteen

"And Liz . . . I forgive you. I understand."

Elizabeth stood by her answering machine, not breathing. She played the message again, hoping she had somehow heard it wrong or was overreacting. But the words that drifted through the dorm room in Jessica's deliriously giddy voice sounded just as ominous—if not more so—the second time. *Going to be with my angel*—what could that possibly mean?

"Please be there, Jess," Elizabeth prayed as she frantically punched in the number of the Wakefield house. "Please don't do anything drastic. Oh God, please."

But the answering machine picked up. Elizabeth practically screamed into the receiver, "Jess, it's me! I'm on my way—*please*, don't do anything until I get there!"

She slammed down the phone and grabbed the

215

keys to the Jeep, a torrent of adrenaline flooding her veins. Every second counted—she cursed her legs for not carrying her fast enough down the stairs and out to the parking lot.

Elizabeth sped home in the Jeep in record time. The road was a blur—and while Elizabeth was usually an extremely cautious driver, today she probably wouldn't have noticed a Mack truck heading straight toward her. All she could think was, *Please let Jessica be OK*. Her twin's face loomed before her in her mind's eye, sad and wan.

Maybe I should have tried harder to listen when she told me about the angel, she berated herself. *Maybe I shouldn't have gone back to campus so soon. Maybe I should have called to tell her about my plan . . . I just didn't want to get her hopes up until I talked to the dean!*

"Oh, Jess," Elizabeth cried, flooring the gas pedal, "if anything happens to you, it's all my fault!"

She pulled up in the Wakefield driveway, tires screeching, and sprinted into the house. "Jessica! Jess! Is anyone home?"

Prince Albert bounded up to Elizabeth, waving his tail excitedly, and followed at her heels as she tore through the hallways, calling Jessica's name. But there was no sign of her sister or her parents.

Elizabeth reached the open door to Jessica's bedroom and felt her knees go weak as she scanned the empty room. Fear churned in her stomach. "Jessica, where are you?" she whispered. She couldn't fathom what her sister might be planning. But she had a strong feeling that if she didn't find Jessica soon, it would be too late.

"Don't get me wrong—Hemingway's style is great," Chloe said, flipping through a volume of the author's short stories. A lock of copper hair fell seductively into her face as she perused the pages. "I'm just turned off by his whole macho trip. After all the stuffy old academies my parents sent me to, I got a little sick of dead white males."

Tom laughed and set down the copy of *The Old Man and the Sea* he was holding. They were seated side by side on a plush red couch in the corner of a quaint bookstore-café, drinking cappuccino. "Well, even us living white males can get a little bored with a writer who thinks a book about fishing is an edge-of-your-seat page-turner."

"Well, it *was* a pretty big fish." Chloe's eyes twinkled with humor. "Tom, this has really been a fun night. I can't *wait* until I'm in college—the guys in my high school would think I was insane if I suggested sitting around and talking about literature."

"Do you think you might end up picking SVU?" It was a conversational question Tom would have asked anyone who was applying to the school, but in the back of his mind he couldn't help wondering seriously if he would ever see Chloe again.

"It depends. I got in early decision, but I haven't made up my mind yet." Chloe's cheeks turned faintly pink. "But if everyone at SVU's as cool as you, I could definitely see myself there."

Tom puffed up his chest. "Well, certainly not *everyone*—I set the bar rather high," he huffed in his best Bruce Patman voice. Chloe doubled over in laughter and put a hand on Tom's knee.

The sensation of her touch and the sound of her laugh were a balm to Tom's self-esteem, which Elizabeth had crushed. It had been a while since a pretty girl flirted with him, and it felt good. *Don't let it go to your head,* he told himself. *She's in high school—she'd probably be impressed by* any *college guy she met.*

Still, they really did have a lot in common—for hours now, they'd been bonding over their shared taste in books, music, movies. Tom couldn't help thinking it would be a treat to run into Chloe on campus next fall.

Chloe glanced at the silver watch on her slender wrist. The spot on Tom's knee where her hand had been still tingled. "Wow, the night flew by. I really should be getting back so I can get up tomorrow—I am *not* a morning person."

Tom stood up and reached out a hand to pull Chloe to her feet. "Your chariot awaits, madam."

On the drive back to the hotel Tom kept

218

glancing over at Chloe, trying to scope out her body language. Would it be presumptuous to make a move?

When they pulled up in front of the hotel, Chloe undid her seat belt but made no move to get out of the car. "Thanks for a wonderful night, Tom."

"The pleasure was all mine." Tom gazed into her shining eyes. Well . . . why not? Her body language was pretty clear. Besides, what if he never got to see her again?

He unbuckled his seat belt, slid across the seat, and kissed Chloe's lips—tentatively at first. But when she responded by wrapping her slim arms around his neck, he kissed her again—and again. . . .

There was a smile on Chloe's face when they untangled. "You should be a recruiter," she said breathily. "The admissions people at Berkeley weren't nearly so convincing."

Tom chuckled. "Well, I hope you'll take into consideration everything SVU has to offer."

"I will. And I'll definitely look you up the next time I'm in town. Good night, Tom." Chloe gave him another soft kiss before sliding out of the car.

Tom watched her disappear through the revolving door of the hotel with a faint, stupid grin on his face. Maybe he'd see Chloe again or maybe not. The important thing was that he was starting to realize there was a wide world of women out there. He didn't have to sit at home nursing his broken heart and wondering where he went wrong. There was life after Elizabeth Wakefield.

Jessica's throat burned from the dry, scratchy pills, but it was a small price to pay. Soon she would be flying through the clouds, soaring weightless through an infinite blue sky. *I can't wait,* she thought dreamily, lifting her next pill to her mouth. She closed her eyes and pictured the angel with Nick's face, his silhouette ringed with golden light.

When she opened her eyes, a black-clad figure was emerging from the trees before her, his shape filling the space where the angel had been. Jessica blinked in confusion, but he didn't disappear. *Am I dreaming? Is it the pills?*

He was approaching fast, treading lightly across the grass. There was something achingly familiar about his gait, the slouch of his shoulders. Jessica caught her breath as he came toward her. *It must be real. It has to be.*

"I knew you'd come," she whispered, standing up and stretching out her arms to him. "I knew you wouldn't leave me."

All at once his fingers laced with hers, their palms pressed together. Jessica felt a surge of energy run through her entire body. Then she stared into his face, half hidden under the brim of a cap, and gasped.

It was him. It had to be him. The beard hid his

chin, and his eyes were mysteriously mud brown . . . but still, she would know that face anywhere.

"Nick?" Jessica whispered, tears filling her eyes. "Is it really you?"

"Annanother thing," Danny said to his new drinking buddy, pointing with a wobbly finger. "Izza-Izzabella doesn't even remember my name. She doesn't even care, man!"

The guy next to Danny, who had identified himself only as Junior, took a swig of his whiskey and rubbed his spiky chin knowingly. "Women never care, kid. They're all heartless."

"Nah, nah, man, Izzabellawazzan like that." Danny rested his elbows on the bar and ran his fingers across his scalp. "She jess . . . she jess couldn't help it 'cause she hurt her head."

Danny knew he was stinking drunk because he could hear the slurring in his own voice—not to mention that the bar was whirling like a top. Yet somehow his head was still as clear, the pain still as vivid and bright, as when he was stone-cold sober. With every breath he took he missed Isabella a little more; with every exhale he felt a little emptier.

Junior took a long drag off a cigarette and regarded Danny through narrowed, bloodshot eyes. "Forget about it, man. Crap happens."

Danny shook his head. "I wish I could. But no madder how mush I drink, I can't forgedder." He drained the last dregs from the empty shot glass before him. "All I wan' is just t' be numb—just t' stop feeling all this horribul schtuff."

"Oh, really?" Junior arched an eyebrow. Smoke drifted out of his nostrils as if he were a dragon. "Well, I might be able to help you out there."

Junior darted almost imperceptible sideways glances in both directions before pulling something from the breast pocket of his grubby denim jacket. He leaned close to Danny, his whiskey breath withering, and uncurled his fist. In his palm was a small, clear plastic bag half full of coarse, brownish white powder.

"Nothing makes the pain go away like this stuff," Junior said in a low, confidential voice. "One hit and you won't remember your own mother's name."

He straightened up and stuffed the plastic bag nonchalantly into his pocket. "If numb's the way you want to go, wait five minutes and meet me in the men's room." Junior clapped Danny on the shoulder before shuffling away.

Danny sat frozen on his bar stool, glancing nervously around to see if anyone else appeared to be on to what was happening. But the other patrons in the bar seemed to be in various stages of unconsciousness. Danny hunkered over his empty shot glass, his mind swimming.

He'd never even considered doing drugs before. It was totally against everything he was about.

But what am *I about now that Isabella's gone?* he asked himself bitterly. All he ever did was get hammered anyway. Doing drugs would just be the next logical step in his career as a total waste of space.

The more he thought about it, the more it seemed oddly appropriate. Smoking PCP was what had caused Isabella's fall and, ultimately, her amnesia. Drugs had made Isabella forget her whole life. . . .

And right now, forgetting was exactly what Danny was desperate to do.

The black-clad man held one of his brown eyes, a wet half circle, on the tip of his finger. Jessica gazed into his face and saw one jade green eye glittering in the light of a nearby street lamp. She gasped sharply.

He replaced the tinted contact lens, and once again both his eyes were a dull, muddy brown. But Jessica could see the light of love shining in them clear as day.

"It's really me, Jessica," his voice, low and urgent, assured her. "I'm sorry it took me so long to find you."

"But how—I must be dreaming. . . ." Jessica trailed off and stared up at him, overwhelmed with emotion. "You're . . . you're . . ."

"Dead? No. I'm real, Jessica. And I'll prove it." He unzipped his padded sweatshirt and reached inside. He produced a scrap of paper on which Jessica recognized her own quickly scrawled handwriting. *Nick,* it read, *I love you. All my love, Jessica.*

"Remember when I was testifying in the Clay DiPalma trial?" he prompted as Jessica stared blankly at the note. "You made the guard pass me this note. I had to destroy the rest of it because of what you said about witnessing DiPalma's confession. But this line I kept."

Jessica slowly lifted her face to his in wonderment. Then the full force of the truth hit her, and she was flooded with relief. She ran her fingers through his hair, slid her palms down his face, yanked at the lapels of his jacket. "Oh, Nick," she cried. "It really *is* you!"

"When I told you I had to enter the witness protection program, you wouldn't accept that we would have to be apart," he explained gently. "I knew as long as you believed I was alive, you would move mountains to find me—and end up putting yourself in danger. I couldn't let that happen."

"So you were just . . . pretending to be dead," Jessica concluded numbly. She buried her face against his chest, deeply inhaling his familiar scent like a drowning victim coming up for air.

"Oh, Jess, if I'd known what it would do to you, I would never have done it." He stroked her hair, holding her tight in his other arm. "I just wanted to protect you—I'd rather be dead for real than see you hurt. Can you ever forgive me?"

"Of course!" Jessica lifted her tear-stained face to his. "Just say we'll be together again, Nick. Now that I know you're alive, you've got to stay with me. You've got to!"

The colored contacts did nothing to mask the pain in his eyes. "I can't," he said throatily. "I'm risking both our lives by even being here. If Clay DiPalma's guys thought for a second that I was alive, much less that I was still in contact with you . . ." He shuddered, his mouth turned down grimly.

"But Nick, I love you so much," Jessica cried. "I don't think I can live without you."

His face softened, but his hands gripped her shoulders tightly. "Yes, you can, Jessica," he assured her. "That's what I love about you." He shook his head and chuckled fondly. "Jess, why do you think I had to fake my own death? Because I know you never give up!"

To her utter surprise, Jessica found herself smiling. She had the strange sensation of recalling the Jessica Wakefield who used to exist—strong willed, indomitable, self-reliant—as if she were a long-lost friend.

"I know it's hard, Jess," he continued intently. "It's hard for me too—you have no idea *how* hard. But I can't stand seeing you like this. All I want is for you to go on with your life, to be happy. Will you do that for me, Jessica?"

"I-I'll try," Jessica promised. Her knees felt weak. Her whole body trembled with the intensity of being so close to him again, the effort of wanting so desperately to memorize everything about this moment.

He spun her around so her back was spooned against his chest and pointed up at the sky. "And Jessica . . . whenever you look up at the moon and the stars, remember that even though I'm somewhere far away, I'm always looking up at that same sky, thinking of you." His voice broke slightly as he buried his face in the nape of Jessica's neck. "I'll always love you, Jessica, as long as I live."

"I love you too, Nick." Jessica's heart swelled, overwhelmed with bittersweet emotion. All of a sudden, being her old self again didn't seem like such a terrifying prospect. As long as he was there with her in spirit . . . maybe she could find the strength to go on.

Jessica's body was slack in his arms. She wanted so much to hold him, to talk to him, to gaze at his beautiful face until it was burned forever in her mind. But her eyelids were heavy, and as hard as she tried, they kept fluttering shut. She fumbled for a hold on his sleeves, but her hands were slipping, hanging at her sides like deadweights. . . .

She was dimly aware of him gently laying her out on the bench. He was holding the box of pills, then pressing it into her hands.

"Good-bye, Jessica." His face hovered over hers, flickering in and out of sight. A cool hand smoothed damp tendrils of hair off her forehead. "I love you."

"Don't go." Jessica moaned with every ounce of her remaining energy, but she knew she didn't have the strength to protest.

The last thing she saw was Nick Fox's face lowering to plant a tender kiss on her lips. She felt the soft pressure of his mouth on hers, and then everything became darkness and silence.

"Jessica!" Elizabeth called out the window of the Jeep. "Jessica, where *are* you?"

It doesn't make sense, she thought, her chest tightening with panic as she rounded another corner. Jessica couldn't have gone far on foot. But how many more times could Elizabeth circle the neighborhood? She'd been at it for hours.

Elizabeth scanned the shadowed sidewalks, her terror mounting. *What if someone picked her up, or . . .* Her mind flitted to the guy who'd been watching Jessica in the Wakefield yard, the guy who *might* have been just a random prowler—or not.

She refused to let herself finish the thought.

Up ahead was a park with a playground where the twins used to play when they were little. Elizabeth slowed down the Jeep as she approached. Jessica had been so nostalgic for old times with Elizabeth . . . would she have sought out one of their old spots? *Well, it's worth a try,* Elizabeth decided, pulling the Jeep up to the curb.

She ran through the line of trees that bordered the park and found herself in a clearing. There was the playground. And there, stretched across the bench, was a motionless human figure . . . with a tangled mane of golden hair hanging almost to the ground.

"Jess-iii-caaa!" Elizabeth didn't recognize the anguished animal cry that escaped her own lips. She kept screaming, her breath coming in quick, hyperventilating gulps, as she raced toward her sister. Elizabeth fell on her knees beside the park bench, sobbing. Jessica's lifeless hands were clutching a silver jewelry box. A peaceful smile was frozen on her lips.

"No!" Elizabeth wailed, beating on the ground with her fists. "No, Jessica, you can't . . ." Seized with frantic, senseless energy, she grabbed her sister by the shoulders and shook desperately. The silver jewelry box slipped from Jessica's grasp and fell open to the ground, empty.

"Jessica, don't go!" Elizabeth wailed. "I need you!" Jessica's head bobbed as Elizabeth kept shaking her shoulders. Then suddenly, miraculously, her eyelashes began to flutter.

Elizabeth released her grip on her sister's shoulders. Sure enough, Jessica was stirring, her mouth stretching lazily into a yawn.

Tears of relief and joy mingled with the tears of

grief that streaked Elizabeth's face. "Jessica!" she cried. "You're alive!"

Jessica's eyes snapped open and fixed on Elizabeth's face. Her mouth stretched into a broad grin. "All right already, Liz. You don't have to shout."

Elizabeth gaped in disbelief at her sister. Jessica's gaze was clear, lucid. Her eyes had lost their glassy, unfocused look. Elizabeth knew instinctively, from the bottom of her heart, that *this* was her twin—not the hollow shell of Jessica who had been wandering helplessly around the Wakefield house for weeks.

Jessica sat up on the bench. "Well, jeez, Liz, aren't you going to give me a hug?" she asked impatiently.

Elizabeth's face cracked into a tearful laugh as she threw her arms around her sister. Jessica returned the hug fiercely. Together they huddled for a long moment in which time stood still, sobbing and laughing at the same time as they clutched each other.

"Jess, I was so scared," Elizabeth whispered into her sister's hair. "I'd be lost without you."

"Same here." Jessica held her sister at arm's length, her gaze shining with pure love. "I should've known you'd never give up on me, Liz."

Elizabeth sniffed. "Of course I wouldn't, Jess. I've been working on helping you get back into school. And I've got great news—wait'll I tell you!"

"OK, Liz, but we should be getting back." Jessica stood up and helped Elizabeth to her feet.

"Mom and Dad must be worried sick. I can't *wait* to tell them how sorry I am for putting them through all this—ha ha."

"You don't have anything to be sorry for," Elizabeth insisted. "But Jess, it's good to have you back."

"It's good to *be* back." Jessica draped an arm across her twin's shoulders.

As they walked arm in arm toward the Jeep, Elizabeth couldn't stop crying, but she couldn't stop smiling either. She had no idea what had happened to pull her sister back from the brink—maybe Jessica would explain when she was ready. But she knew that no matter how long it took, no matter how much love and support and encouragement her sister needed, Jessica was on the road to recovery. And Elizabeth knew that with her help, Jessica would get there. Together they could accomplish anything.

When he cleared a safe distance from the park, he slowed his run to a stop and leaned against a tree, panting. His rib cage felt as if it were about to burst from the stitch in his side, but he didn't care. All that mattered was that it was all over. He'd done what he had to do.

Jessica will pull through, he told himself. He knew it in his heart. There was no way he could have mistaken the old spark in her eyes—he knew her too well.

Cautiously he stepped out from behind the tree and walked over to a nearby sewer grate. He stretched out his palm and quickly dumped out the handful of sedatives he was holding. Luckily he'd reached her in time—she'd only taken two, maybe three before she spotted him. He prayed Jessica would never have to endure such a close call again.

He wiped his clammy hands on his pant legs and reached into his jacket. His fingertips found the shred of Jessica's love note in the pocket where he always kept it—close to his heart.

I can move on now, he realized, a strange sense of emptiness mingling with his relief. *Jessica's safe . . . but I'll never see her again.*

With a heavy heart, Nick Fox set off again down the street. Finally he could start his new life—but it would be a bleak, empty one without Jessica.

At least I'll always cherish the memory of kissing her one last time, Nick consoled himself. And as he rounded a corner in the darkness, that's exactly what Nick Fox became . . . a memory.

Elizabeth, Jessica, and all their friends at SVU are headed for adventure this summer—and starting a new year in the fall! Fresh faces and new friendships are on the horizon as the students of SVU take another step toward total freedom—and it all starts with Sweet Valley University #48: **NO RULES.** *Don't miss it!*

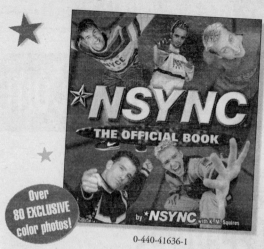